Murder at the Masquerade

THE REBECCA ORANGE CASTLE COZY MYSTERY SERIES

BOOK SIX

VALERIE BRANDY

EMERALD LION PRESS

Published by: Emerald Lion Press. 23901 Calabasas Rd., Ste 2088, Calabasas, CA 91302. emeraldlionpress@gmail.com

ISBN: 978-1-964161-81-5

Editing provided by Sharon Lennon-Mehlschau.

Printed in the United States of America. To request permission to use passages from this book in any context other than a review, please contact the publisher at emeraldlionpress@gmail.com.

Visit the author's website at: www.valeriebrandy.com

 Formatted with Vellum

CHAPTER

One

"THIS WEDDING TRADITION might actually be worse than Monrovian bridesmaids' hats," I mutter to Maggie, adjusting the mask strapped across my face. Feathers stick out from the edges and tangle in my hair. I reach up to scratch my nose. A rogue panel of beading across the mask's nose-piece makes me feel like I'm about to sneeze, but I resist.

Somewhere behind us, castle staff string the last of the olive-branch garlands shot through with warm twinkle lights onto the wall sconces. The garlands are a Monrovian Halloween— or "All Souls Day," as they call it here— staple. Nearby, a row of charming carved pumpkins wait to be carried downstairs. Their candlelit grins flicker orange against the stone.

"Oh, hush," Maggie laughs, tightening the band on the back of my mask until it perches just right. She's wearing her own disguise— a pearl-encrusted mask that covers her face from forehead to chin. "The wedding masquerade is a Monrovian *classic*! Little girls dream of the day they get to throw their own masquerade to announce their engagement."

"Can I donate mine to one of them?" I ask, giving an

ironic twirl in my enormous midnight-blue ballgown. "I'm sure they'd appreciate it more."

"I hope not!" Maggie says, laughing. "Masquerades are only for brides with an *impending* wedding. Don't you see how fun it is? It's a tradition that goes back centuries. The entire village would gather in masks and try to guess who the bride was..."

"I know, I know." I wave a hand dismissively. "Jack explained it already. I still don't get why *I* have to have a big party. Lady Harriet didn't have a masquerade."

"Lady Harriet cleverly disappeared from public life for years," Maggie says. "She got away with skipping the fuss. You and the Duke, unfortunately, are still front and center. Until he abdicates and runs off to open an animal sanctuary with you, you're stuck indulging our weirdest traditions."

"Running off to operate an animal sanctuary? Honestly, not a bad idea." I glance at my reflection in a full-length mirror propped against the wall. I'm swallowed in layers of fabric, the dress ballooning around my hips like an upside-down bell. The mask hides my forehead, nose, and upper eyes, and my hair is tucked under a massive powdered wig the color of stale meringue. The whole look is so far removed from my usual style, I hardly recognize myself. "I could wear sweatpants there."

I don't mention that Jack and I have been quietly wondering where we fit in Monrovian society after the wedding. Late at night in the castle library, we've spent hours trying to plan for the future. But the planning always circles back to the same questions: *How* should we get married? *When*? Jack feels obligated to hold a public wedding in the name of royal transparency and service. Me? I'd rather stand barefoot on a riverbank with Joe at my side and no dress code in sight. Our visions are so different, we haven't planned much of anything yet—except for this engagement masquerade.

"It's a good omen that your masquerade is the same month as 'All Souls Day'!" Maggie says, smiling at me.

"You mean *Halloween*?" I laugh, teasing her. We've been fighting about the proper name for the day, which— in my home country— is all about candy and trick-or-treating.

"You Americans and your candy," Maggie shakes her head. "This month is deeper than treats." She leans in, making a ghostly twitching motion with her fingers. "October is when we thin the veil between this world and the beyond. It's a special time to have a wedding masquerade. Very auspicious." Maggie opens the door and gestures toward the hallway. Olive-leaf and tiny-lantern garlands loop between the sconces, each lantern painted with miniature gold suns for the living and silver moons for the departed— Monrovians use the month leading up to All Souls Day to light the way for ancestors.

"I'm still going to call it Halloween just to annoy you," I say, sticking my tongue out at Maggie, who returns the gesture.

"Ready to make your debut?" Maggie asks. Beside her, Joe barks in agreement. He's wearing a mask of his own— dark blue with yellow scrollwork around the edges, a feather drooping over one ear. Benjamin at *L'Animalerie Indiana Bones* hand-crafted it, of course.

"Alright," I sigh. "Let's get this over with."

The three of us step into the castle's stone hallway, my heart pounding. At this party, every guest descends the grand staircase and has their anonymous presence announced by the Royal Guard—another delightfully obnoxious Monrovian custom.

"How long until I can see Jack?" I whisper.

"He enters separately from you," Maggie says softly, the flickering sconces catching the pearls in her hair. "Otherwise, they'd guess you're the bride. You'll find him in the ballroom. Don't worry. Until then, you've got us."

She points at Joe, giving him the signal to bark. He obliges.

"See? Joe says you're going to have fun and stop fretting about everything."

"I hate that you've memorized all my training signals," I grumble with a laugh. "You're too good at using Joe's cuteness against me."

We turn a corner and arrive at the top of the grand staircase leading down into the castle's royal ballroom. Halloween garlands twirl around each banister post, and small carved pumpkins— some bearing ornate family crests— glow on every step. A velvet runner lines the stairs, spilling into the scene below. Hundreds of masked guests swirl through the room, unrecognizable behind their disguises. A live band plays in the corner while caterers weave through the crowd with trays.

At the base of the stairs, a member of the Royal Guard bangs a metal gong. Conversations fall silent. All eyes turn to the staircase.

"Announcing, a new arrival!" the guard bellows, his voice echoing.

Maggie whistles for Joe. He trots forward, standing next to the guard just like we practiced.

"I'm so glad we let Joe enter first," Maggie whispers. "Otherwise, he'd give you away immediately."

Joe sits at attention, staring expectantly at the guard.

"Introducing... Monsieur Tout-le-Monde!" the guard proclaims.

Maggie explained earlier that "Monsieur Tout-le-Monde" means *Mr. Everyone*. Every guest is introduced as Mr. or Mrs. everyone. It's a way to preserve the masquerade's anonymity.

Applause ripples through the room. Joe takes this as his cue and trots down the stairs into the crowd, tail wagging, utterly unbothered by the hundreds of masked faces.

Next up is Maggie. She squeezes my hand. "You're going to do great," she whispers, then steps forward.

The guard bangs the gong again. "Madame Tout-le-Monde!" he announces.

The guests applaud as Maggie descends, twirling her dress. She moves like someone who enjoys the chance to vanish into a temporary identity—free to be the center of attention without any consequences.

My turn.

I step forward, hands clenched tightly in my skirts. The guard strikes the gong once more, and all eyes lift to me.

"Madame Tout-le-Monde!" he shouts.

Hundreds of masked faces stare. Somewhere in the crowd, they're all wondering the same thing: *Which one of these women is Rebecca Orange?*

I take a breath and step onto the top stair. My mind races. How can I walk in a way that doesn't give me away? People are looking for someone who walks like *me*. So... how would *not me* walk?

My palms are damp. My heart pounds. Every instinct screams at me to run back to my room and hide under the covers.

And then—

The lights go out.

The castle plunges into darkness. The only specks of light come from the Halloween garlands tracing the banister. Their battery-operated twinkle-lights hang suspended in the darkness like fireflies, but it's not enough to see the room.

From below, I hear the clatter of a dropped tray, followed by a scream. Voices murmur nervously through the dark.

Just as suddenly, the lights flicker back on. Guests shuffle in confusion, glancing around.

My eyes take in the newly lit space, looking for what's changed. I spot Joe in Maggie's arms— he's jumped up in fright. She's trying to hold him, though his back legs are still on the floor because he weighs too much. She gives me a thumbs-up to tell me he's okay— just scared. Joe's always been afraid of the dark.

Then— another scream.

"He's dead!" a voice shouts.

Gasps ripple through the ballroom. Guests stumble back, leaving a wide circle around a man sprawled on the floor.

He's wearing a suit and a mask. A knife juts from his chest. Blood pools beneath him. I recognize the salt-and-pepper gray hair on his head.

Panic floods my limbs. I rush down the stairs, heart hammering, every step faster than the last.

Please, don't let it be Jack.

CHAPTER

Two

"IT'S NOT HIM." The words tumble from my lips, a desperate prayer finally answered as I stare down at the body sprawled across the ballroom floor. My fingers tremble as they reach for the ornate Venetian mask still secured to the dead man's face. All around me, the sounds of the masquerade ball have dissolved into gasps and whispers, but I barely register them. All I can think is: *Thank God it's not Jack.*

I bend down, my heart racing so fast I can feel it in my throat. The man lies motionless on his back, arms splayed at unnatural angles. His costume— a classic black tuxedo with tails—is nearly identical to what Jack had chosen to wear tonight. The elaborate silver mask covers most of his face, leaving only his mouth visible, lips slightly parted as if in mid-sentence. His salt and pepper hair is so similar to Jack's that it sends a chill up my spine. The resemblance between the two men is uncanny.

"Excuse me," I murmur to no one in particular as I reach for the edge of the mask. My fingers connect with cool porcelain, and I gently lift it away from the man's face. The resemblance to Jack is there—the same distinguished jawline, similar nose—but the differences are immediately apparent too. This man's features are softer, his face slightly rounder. His eyes, frozen open in what looks like surprise, are hazel, not the deep brown I've grown to love.

I let out a big sigh as I tell myself the truth, again: *It's not him.*

"Ma'am, please step back." A member of the Royal Guard is trying to pull me away. His voice barely registers as I continue to stare at the dead man's face.

The ballroom around me feels impossibly large now, the ceiling too high, the chandeliers too bright. Just thirty minutes ago, this room was where Jack and I were going to celebrate our engagement. Now it will be remembered as a murder scene.

I rise to my feet, and the corset in my gown pinches me. See, Maggie? I think. This is why I prefer sweatpants. I've never been good with formal events, but I'd been making an effort tonight, trying to fit into Jack's world. And now this.

"Rebecca!" Jack's voice makes me melt. The world seems to sit right on its axis. He appears at my side, still wearing his own mask pushed up on top of his head. His hand finds mine and squeezes, the pressure grounding me back to reality. "Leave us, please. That's an order," the Duke says to the member of the Royal Guard, who backs off immediately.

Jack's hands circle my waist as he scans me top to bottom. "Are you alright?" He whispers, the words meant only for me. "The lights went out and— well, of course I knew it was you on the stairs… you have such a distinct walk!"

A distinct walk?

"We're going to circle back to the 'distinct walk' thing," I tell him, although I know exactly what he means. I've been told my walk is more of a skip. "I'm so relieved," I say, leaning into him. "The man who was stabbed— I thought he was you."

"Me?" Jack says, surprised. "No, I was over by the dessert

table, I'm afraid. Right where you'd expect to find— Did you say… stabbed?" It seems as if Jack is only just noticing the man on the floor beside us. He steps back, looking at the body. His face flushes. "My God."

"I know," I say, shaking my head sadly. "He looks just like you!"

"Well, yes, but that's not why I'm—" Jack stammers. "That's Ambassador Franklin. The representative from Antanaro. He'd been here for work and I invited him to our engagement party and now…"

"He's dead," I say, lacking tact.

"If I'd known his life was in danger I never would have invited him," Jack says, clearly reeling from the gruesome news.

We stand there for a moment, an island of stillness in the sea of chaos the ballroom has become. The Royal Guard tries to clear a space around the body. At the edge of the room, I see Maggie still holding on to Joe, Benjamin from the pet store by her side. Guests in their elaborate costumes mill about, some crying, others frantically making phone calls. The orchestra members stand awkwardly by their abandoned instruments, as if unsure whether they should pack up or play a requiem.

"Everyone FREEZE!"

The commanding voice cuts through the noise like a knife. A woman in a flowing emerald ball gown strides forward, her matching mask now clutched in one hand while the other holds up a badge. At first, I don't recognize her, but then, I realize I'm looking at the sturdy frame of Officer Basilier. Even without her uniform, there's no mistaking that authoritative air she has. It's one that screams "I have a stun gun I can't wait to use."

She reaches us and gives me a curt nod of recognition before addressing the room at large. "I am Officer Basilier with the Monrovian Police." She projects her voice without shouting, a skill I've always envied. "This is now an active crime scene. All guests are ordered to proceed to the adjacent reception halls immediately. Castle staff will direct you. No one leaves the premises without being interviewed."

As she speaks, I notice Joe has escaped Maggie's clutches and appeared at my side. My faithful Tibetan Mastiff dog can always sense when I need him. He presses his warm, solid weight against my leg, a living anchor in this surreal moment. I rest my hand on his massive head.

"Duke Atwood," Officer Basilier says, turning to Jack, "I'll need your assistance with coordinating the Royal Guard, if they're willing?"

"Of course," Jack nods. "Anything you need I'll order them to provide.

Her eyes shift to me. "And Rebecca, I imagine you'll want to be involved in this."

"I'm so glad you want my help!" I exclaim. Officer Basilier and I have reached an uneasy friendship lately. It's a nice change from our initial mutual loathing.

"I didn't say I *want* your help," she corrects me, rolling her eyes. "I said obviously you and Maggie will want to be involved and I'll allow it."

Jack squeezes my hand one more time before releasing it. "I'll help get the guests settled," he says, his voice shifting into what I privately call his "Duke mode"— calm, authoritative, reassuring. "It seems the Royal Investigators have work to do." He winks at me before walking toward the Captain of the Royal Guard. I know he'll order them to help Officer Basilier. Jack is always looking for ways to help.

Officer Basilier nods, then turns back to address the stunned crowd. "Move in an orderly fashion. Leave your contact details with the staff. Anyone with information about what happened here tonight, please identify yourself to an officer."

As the guests begin to file out, I take one last look at the dead man on the floor. Ambassador Franklin. Who would want to kill an Ambassador? And why tonight, at my wedding masquerade?

Joe nudges my hand with his nose, bringing me back to the present. Together, we follow Officer Basilier and Jack, leaving behind the glittering ballroom that, in the span of a few minutes, has transformed from a scene of celebration to one of death.

———

The ballroom looks different now, emptied of its glittering crowd. What remains is a hollow shell of the celebration— abandoned champagne flutes, a scatter of dropped masks, and that incongruous body still lying where it fell. Joe stays close to my side as Officer Basilier leads our small group— me, Maggie, Jack, and herself— in a slow circle around the corpse. The hem of her emerald ball gown sweeps the marble floor as she walks, and I can't stop staring at her. I've seen Officer Basilier take charge of crime scenes before, but never while dressed like she's auditioning for a royal court.

"All guests are in the east and west reception halls," Maggie reports, her tablet in hand despite her elaborate costume. Her efficiency never ceases to amaze me. "I've got staff taking contact information, and the kitchen is serving tea and refreshments to keep everyone calm."

"Good work," Officer Basilier nods, then catches me staring at her again. "For God's sake, Orange, take a picture. It'll last longer."

I feel my cheeks flush. "Sorry, it's just—"

"Just what? Never seen a woman in a dress before?" She raises an eyebrow, the gesture somehow more intimidating with her full makeup and styled hair.

"Never seen you in one," I admit. "It's like seeing a tiger in a tutu."

Jack coughs to cover what I suspect is a laugh. Officer Basilier narrows her eyes at me, but there's a glimmer of amusement there.

"Well, I'm glad I can finally stop trying to be you," she says, gesturing to her costume. "I won't lie Miss Orange. I was offended by the number of guests who tried to identify me as the bride. Apparently you and I share a similar walk."

"We're both very purposeful with our steps," I agree. "Although I'd like to think my walk is a little… jauntier?"

Officer Basilier lets out a *hrumph* sound that tells me she very much doubts it.

"Regardless, I was very much looking forward to a simple night out. But so much for that. Should have known better than to attend the same event as you, Orange. Corpses follow you like lost puppies."

Joe lets out a small whine, as if offended on behalf of puppies everywhere.

"So," I say, eager to change the subject, "what do we know so far?"

Officer Basilier's face instantly transforms from teasing to professional. " The Victim is Ambassador Franklin of Antanaro. Time of death approximately 9:30 PM, during the second orchestral set. Cause appears to be stabbing…"

No kidding, I think, staring at the knife in his chest.

"But despite the obvious weapon," Officer Basilier continues, "We're having toxicology test him anyway. Just in case."

I glance down at the man's face again. Ambassador Franklin.

"I knew him well," Jack says softly. "He's been Antanaro's Ambassador to Monrovia for over a decade. Wouldn't hurt a fly. It was my fault he was here," Jack adds shakily. "I was telling Rebecca I should never have invited him."

Officer Basilier clicks her pen loudly and takes notes in her journal. I can't help but raise an eyebrow at her. "Jack is not a suspect," I say hastily, thinking of a past murder in which Officer Basilier was convinced Jack was the culprit.

Officer Basilier scoffs. "You're never going to let that go, are you?" She rolls her eyes. "Arrest a man *one time* and I'm forever blacklisted… Honestly, Orange, I thought we were friends now."

Friends. The word is a shocking one, coming from Officer Basilier. I resist the urge to hug her and instead play it cool, turning back to Jack.

"Did the Ambassador have any enemies that you know of?" I ask.

Jack shakes his head. "None. He was well-liked, even during tense diplomatic moments. A quiet, kind man. Easy to get along with."

"It's all over the news that Monrovia and Antanaro are in dispute over Île des Lilas," Officer Basilier interjects smoothly. "Is that why he was here?"

"Île des Lilas?" I ask, struggling to translate. "The Island of … ?"

"The Island of Lilacs," Maggie says, helping me make the leap. "It's been all over Jack's calendar this month," she adds, ignoring the warning look from Jack.

"Yes," Jack admits. "The Ambassador was here to discuss resolution of the island ownership problem. It's a small but strategically located isle between Monrovia and Antanaro. There's been debate over ownership for years, but despite what the press reports, we've reached an agreement in principle. The Royal Council votes this week on a proposal for shared ownership—split 50/50 with Antanaro."

The Island of Lilacs. Suddenly, I remember I've heard the name on the news as well. "Nobody lives there though, right?" I say stupidly.

"It's mostly uninhabited," Jack agrees. "But for a research station and a place for ships to get supplies. That's the real sticking point, though. It's a useful little place, given its location is right where ships need it most."

"And you're voting in favor of shared ownership?" Officer Basilier asks.

"I am," Jack confirms. "It's the right solution. The island has historical significance to both nations, and shared stewardship makes the most sense economically and culturally."

I look down at the dead Ambassador, a cold feeling settling in my stomach. "How will his death affect the vote?"

Maggie speaks up, her political instincts sharp as ever. "It could complicate things. Some might see it as a reason to postpone. Others might use it as leverage to push for full Monrovian control, claiming Antanaro can't be trusted."

"Or," I add, "some might think Monrovia had him killed to create exactly that scenario."

Jack shudders at the idea, running a hand through his hair, a gesture I've come to recognize as a sign of his concern. "This couldn't have happened at a worse time."

Officer Basilier clears her throat. "While the political fallout is interesting, I'm more concerned with finding a killer." She moves to the body and points to the Ambassador's right hand, which is partially closed around something. "We found this clutched in his fist. Appears he grabbed it during a struggle with his attacker."

I lean closer to see a small swatch of bright yellow fabric, dotted with gold sequins that catch the light from the chandeliers above.

"Fabric from a costume," I murmur.

"Exactly," Officer Basilier nods. "Based on our preliminary review of the guest list and staff observations, we've identified five individuals wearing costumes with this specific yellow sequined material." She straightens up, the movement somehow dignified despite her elaborate gown. "We need to question them immediately."

"Any of them have motive?" Jack asks.

"That's what we need to find out," Officer Basilier replies. She turns to Maggie and me. "Since you two insist on playing detective with your 'Royal Investigators' side hustle, I suppose you might as well make yourselves useful. Care to assist with the interrogations?"

Maggie's eyes light up with excitement. "Absolutely!"

"Interrogations are a bit much for a castle ballroom, don't you think?" I say, glancing around at the gilded mirrors and crystal chandeliers. "Maybe we could call them 'interviews with persons of interest'?"

"Call them tea parties if you want, Orange," Officer Basilier retorts, a hint of a smile playing at her lips. "As long as we find out who killed the Ambassador."

Joe nudges my hand with his cold nose, reminding me of his presence. I scratch behind his ears, grateful for his presence. Luma—Jack's dog, and Joe's de facto best friend— had planned on joining us tonight but tired herself chasing geese by the pond. Right now, she's probably happily asleep on Jack's bed.

"Alright," I say, straightening my shoulders and trying to look as professional as one can in a Renaissance gown. "Let's find our five suspects and see what they have to say for themselves."

Maggie is already tapping on her tablet. "I'll have them brought to a room for questioning."

As our small group prepares to split up for the interviews, I take one last look at Ambassador Franklin lying on the ballroom floor. Someone in this castle ended his life tonight. And whether the motive was personal or political, I intend to find out who— and why.

CHAPTER
Three

THE CASTLE LIBRARY *feels too small for this many egos* I think, taking in our esteemed guests. I stand near the doorway, watching as Officer Basilier arranges our five suspects on separate sofas and chairs among the towering bookshelves. The library has been decorated for the season, and miniature pumpkins rest on the mantle of the fireplace. In another corner, books on "All Souls Day" and its history are featured in a prominent position.

Joe presses against my leg, his massive bulk a comforting presence as I take in the scene before me— five suspects sit on the couches, connected by sequined fabric and a dead Ambassador. Maggie catches my eye from across the room, her expression a mixture of excitement and determination. Neither of us say it aloud, but I know we're thinking the same thing: the Royal Investigators are officially on the case.

"Please, be seated," Officer Basilier instructs me and Maggie, gesturing to two vacant wingback chairs. She's changed out of her ball gown into her police uniform, which makes this night feel less surreal. I like seeing Officer Basilier dressed like her normal self.

I take a moment to study our suspects as Joe and I move toward our designated seats. Before we entered the room, Maggie pulled up pictures on her tablet and gave me a rundown of who we're dealing with. Now, I'm mentally matching the pictures to the real-life versions in front of me.

The woman with the perfect posture and even more perfect cheekbones is instantly recognizable. She's Missy Adeline, the Antanaran movie star whose face graces billboards across Europe. *She's prettier in person,* I think, making a mental note not to say as much.

Beside her sits a slender man in a paisley shirt who keeps checking his phone— I recognize him as her publicist, a man Maggie told me goes by only one name: Sacks. *One name? I asked Maggie as she showed me his photo. Who does he think he is? Oprah?*

My eyes move on from Sacks to the opposite sofa, where a plump man with an impressive mustache shifts impatiently. His knee bounces with nervous energy. This is the Prime Minister Floridán, who serves as the head of the Monrovian parliament. He's a powerful man who looks thoroughly annoyed to be here. Next to him sits a plain-faced woman in sensible shoes who I assume is his wife, Geneviève.

Please don't let one of them be the murderer I think, imagining the amount of political turmoil such a thing would cause for Jack.

I move on to a nearby ottoman, where a well-dressed woman with clever eyes is perched, studying everyone in the room— this is the dressmaker, Ms. Labelle. She looks older than the picture Maggie showed me, but I recognize her at once by her modest, long face.

"What is THAT doing here?" the movie star, Missy Adeline, suddenly exclaims, pointing a manicured finger at Joe, who has settled at my feet with a soft huff.

"That," I reply, resting my hand on Joe's massive head, "is Joe. He's a part of the Royal Investigators team."

"A dog can't be a part of anything except a mess," Missy Adeline says. Her perfect eyebrows arch so high they nearly disappear into her hairline. I'm liking her less and less.

I won't be going to see a single one of your movies after this, I think as loudly as possible.

"Joe is a highly trained Tibetan Mastiff with more investigative experience than most humans," I say, trying to keep my voice even. "He's been instrumental in solving several cases."

Sacks— Missy's publicist– leans forward, his paisley shirt catching the light in a way that makes my eyes hurt. "You expect us to believe this... *animal* ...is a detective?"

Joe chooses this moment to sit up straighter, somehow looking more dignified than half the humans in the room. Joe's been trained to perform a variety of behaviors, and in our previous cases, I've discovered he has an uncanny ability to sense when something's off.

"Joe has exceptional observational skills," I explain, which isn't technically a lie. "His presence here is non-negotiable."

"How fascinating," Ms. Labelle comments, her voice warm with genuine interest. "I've read about service animals, but never a detective dog."

Officer Basilier clears her throat. "If we're quite finished discussing the dog's credentials," she says with barely concealed impatience, "I'd like to move on to the murder investigation."

The word "murder" silences the room immediately.

"I've gathered you all here because you share something in common," Officer Basilier continues, reaching into her pocket and removing a small evidence bag. Inside is the scrap of yellow sequined fabric we found clutched in Ambassador Franklin's hand. She holds it up, the gold sequins catching the light. "This was found in the victim's hand. We believe it tore from the killer's costume during a struggle."

Ms. Labelle gasps, her hand flying to her mouth. "That's

—" She stops herself, then takes a deep breath. "That's my fabric."

All eyes turn to her.

"Go on," Officer Basilier prompts, even though I suspect she already knows where this is heading.

"Yes," Ms. Labelle nods, her composure returning. "I ordered that specific sequined material from Paris. It's quite distinctive— a particular shade of yellow with these unique gold sequins that catch the light differently depending on the angle." She reaches for her purse, a small clutch sitting beside her, and holds it up. It's made from the same vibrant yellow material. "I made something for each person in this room using that exact fabric."

The room falls silent again, this time with a heavier weight.

"Can everyone confirm?" Maggie speaks up for the first time, her voice calm and measured, "Raise your hand if you're wearing an item that's made from this fabric."

Every hand in the room raises, except Prime Minister Floridán. His wife elbows him in the ribs and finally, he raises his hand.

"Yes," Ms. Labelle confirms. "The fabric was a special order, very expensive. I only had enough for a few pieces."

Officer Basilier turns to Missy Adeline. "Let's start with you, Ms. Adeline. What item did Ms. Labelle make for you?"

The movie star tosses her hair back dramatically. "My gown, of course. The yellow sequined masterpiece I wore tonight." She sighs as if greatly put upon. "My publicist, Sacks, suggested I have something made locally, even though Antanaro's dressmakers are far superior to anyone in Monrovia."

I catch the slight flinch from Ms. Labelle at these words.

"I put my standards aside for one night," Missy continues. She looks around expectantly, apparently waiting for someone to acknowledge her charitable work.

"And why did you suggest local work, Mr. Sacks?" Officer Basilier asks, moving on without giving Missy the validation she clearly wants.

Sacks crosses his legs, revealing socks that match his paisley shirt. "It's just Sacks, no 'Mister,'" he corrects with a hint of condescension. "And it was purely a public relations decision. Local press loves when international celebrities support local businesses." He gestures toward Ms. Labelle. "I heard about her shop from other clients who raved about her work."

"And you picked up a little something for yourself, I see?" Officer Basilier nods at Sacks' shirt.

Sacks shrugs. "Why not? There was left over fabric so I got myself something pretty." He winks at Officer Basilier, and I see her right hand twitch. I'm pretty sure she's fighting the urge to reach for her stun gun.

I study Sacks' shirt. It's primarily made of a cheaper paisley fabric, but yellow sequined accents run along the collar and cuffs, matching his socks. The overall effect is gaudy, but I suppose it makes a statement.

"This is ridiculous!" Prime Minister Floridán suddenly erupts, his mustache quivering with indignation. "Why are my wife and I being subjected to this... this inquisition? We have nothing to do with this tragic event!"

"Prime Minister," I say before Officer Basilier can respond, my voice deliberately calm, "if you truly have nothing to hide, then wouldn't it be wise to let the police do their job? Cooperating fully would be the fastest way to clear your name... don't you think?"

His face reddens, but before he can retort, his wife places a gentle hand on his arm.

"The *future duchess* is absolutely right, dear," Gineviève says softly. The way she emphasized the words "future duchess" makes me think she's trying to make a point to her husband. Her voice is surprisingly authoritative despite its quiet tone. "As representatives of Monrovia, we should set an example of full transparency."

The Prime Minister deflates slightly, his bluster fading under his wife's measured reason.

"We're happy to explain our attire," Geneviève continues, addressing Officer Basilier directly. "I chose that particular yellow fabric for my dress because it's one of Monrovia's national colors. It seemed appropriate to incorporate patriotic elements into our formal wear tonight." She gestures to her husband. "I also had a matching tie made for my husband."

Missy Adeline lets out an audible huff. "So not only do I have to share fabric with some... politician's wife, but you intentionally copied Antanaro's color scheme?"

"Yellow is Monrovia's color as well," Geneviève responds evenly. "It represents the golden beaches along our coastline."

"It represents the sunrise over Antanaro's mountains first!" Missy snaps back.

As they bicker over national color ownership, I exchange glances with Maggie. Five suspects, five items made from the same fabric, and one dead Ambassador. Somewhere in this tangle of yellow sequins and oversized egos lies the truth about what happened to Ambassador Franklin tonight. But it's clear— our guests aren't in the mood to cooperate. This is going to take some digging.

Officer Basilier seems to feel the same, because she rises from her seat, her posture straight as a ruler. "Thank you all for your cooperation," she says, though her tone suggests she found their answers anything but cooperative. "You're free to return to your rooms, but I must insist that no one leaves Monrovia until this investigation is complete." Five pairs of eyes widen at this news, and I can practically hear the mental calculations of canceled appointments and rescheduled flights. The politics of murder, it turns out, are nothing compared to the politics of inconvenienced schedules.

"This is outrageous!" Missy Adeline exclaims, her perfect features contorting in horror. "I have a film premiere in Paris next week!"

"And I have a country to run," Prime Minister Floridán adds, his mustache practically vibrating with indignation. His wife, Geneviève, puts a hand on his knee.

"But of course," she adds. "We were planning on staying the weekend anyway. We can do our best to be available for your investigation during our holiday."

"Thank you," Officer Basilier nods.

Maggie steps forward smoothly, her tablet already in hand. "Rest assured, we'll make your extended stay as comfortable as possible," she says in that soothing tone that somehow makes even the most unreasonable requests sound perfectly reasonable. "For those of you staying at the castle—" she glances at Ms. Labelle, the only one who lives in the village "—we'll ensure your rooms remain available, and any special requirements you have will be accommodated."

One by one, our suspects file out of the library. Ms. Labelle leaves first, promising to be available at her shop tomorrow for further questions. She seems genuinely shaken, clutching her yellow sequined purse like it might bite her. The Prime Minister and his wife follow, his face still flushed with anger while she maintains that calculating calm that makes me think she's already three steps ahead of everyone else in the room. Missy Adeline makes a dramatic exit, pausing at the door to inform us all that her lawyer will be contacting "someone important" about this treatment. Sacks trails behind her, still tapping away at his phone, perhaps already crafting the press release about how his client is bravely cooperating with authorities.

When the door finally closes behind them, leaving just Officer Basilier, Maggie, Joe and me, I exhale slowly. "Well, that was productive."

"About as productive as trying to milk a rooster," Officer Basilier mutters, dropping into a chair. "But it's a start." She looks between Maggie and me with calculating eyes. "Now, about your Royal Investigators business..."

"We prefer 'service,'" Maggie corrects gently. "Royal Investigators Service."

"Whatever you call it," Officer Basilier continues, "I need your help. You two have access to this castle and its occupants in ways my officers don't. People talk to you."

I raise an eyebrow. "You're including us because you *want* us here?"

"Don't look so smug, Orange," she replies, a rare smile crossing her lips. "After the Fantasia Rivers case, we both know I'd be a fool not to use your...particular talents."

"By 'particular talents,' do you mean my natural charm and wit?" I ask innocently.

"I mean your annoying ability to get people to tell you things they shouldn't," she says dryly. "And your knack for sticking your nose where it doesn't belong but somehow finding important clues anyway."

"I'll take that as a compliment," I say, scratching Joe behind the ears. He looks up at me with those soulful eyes that always seem to say, "what's next, Mom?"

"What should we focus on?" Maggie asks, already making notes on her tablet.

Officer Basilier leans forward. "Background on all five suspects. Their movements tonight, who they talked to, any connections to Ambassador Franklin or to the island dispute. I want to know if anyone had a reason to want him dead."

"And you think the killer is one of those five?" I ask.

"The fabric evidence suggests it," she says. "Unless someone else at the ball was wearing that exact yellow sequined material that we haven't identified yet."

"I can get the complete guest list and cross-reference it with the staff who observed costumes," Maggie offers.

"Good," Officer Basilier nods. "And look into the politics too. This couldn't have happened at a worse time with that island vote this week."

The weight of the situation suddenly feels heavier. This isn't just about finding a murderer—it's about preventing a diplomatic crisis between two nations. If Antanaro believes Monrovia was behind their Ambassador's death, years of careful negotiation could unravel overnight. And if the media gets hold of the story with all its political implications...

"We need to work fast," I say, voicing what we're all thinking. "Before this turns into an international incident."

Officer Basilier stands, straightening her uniform. "I'll have forensics results by tomorrow afternoon. We'll reconvene here to compare notes." She hesitates, then adds, "And Orange? Try not to cause a scene."

"When have I ever done that?" I ask innocently.

She gives me a look that could wither a cactus. "The giraffe nearly sitting on a murderer—"

"That worked!" I protest.

"The interruption of a celebration for the crown jewels. A high-profile chase by the fountain involving two dogs..."

"In my defense, these scenarios all led to catching the killer," I counter.

"Just... be subtle," she sighs, heading for the door. "And keep that mountain of fur under control." She gestures to Joe, who responds by wagging his tail enthusiastically, apparently taking her insult as a compliment.

After she leaves, Maggie and I look at each other in silence for a moment.

"So," Maggie finally says, "the game is afoot?"

"Technically, it's 'apaw,'" I correct, nodding toward Joe, who's now stretched out on the library carpet looking more like a bear rug than a detective.

Maggie groans at my terrible pun, but she's smiling.

"Let's get some sleep," I suggest, patting Joe's massive head. "Tomorrow, we hunt for a killer."

We walk with confidence, but as the three of us leave the castle library, I can't shake the feeling that this case is different. Somewhere in this castle, behind one of these many doors, a murderer is watching us, wondering if we'll discover their secret before it's too late.

CHAPTER
Four

THE FIREPLACE in my staff apartment crackles with a comforting snap that feels like a hug after the events of the day. I'm back in my sweatpants— my ballgown has been tossed into the bottom of my closet, where it belongs. Jack sits across from me in an old leather chair, a teacup looking too small in his hand. Joe and Luma are sprawled together near the hearth, their bodies intertwined in canine contentment. A tray of pumpkin cookies sits on the table between us, glittering white icing carving faces on their surfaces. The cookies are one of Chef Renauld's seasonal treats.

"See, this is why I don't like big events for weddings," I say, reaching for one of the cookies. They're still warm, the icing melting slightly against my fingers. "The masquerade was like a test run. Our first official engagement event, and someone gets murdered. If we keep going with this, who knows what could happen, or how many people could die!"

Jack laughs, taking a sip of his cinnamon-turmeric latte. The foam on top was originally drawn in the shape of a single candy corn, but now it's a muddled mess. "Are you calling our wedding a serial killer?"

"I'm saying it has the potential to be one," I confirm,

nodding at the silver tray between us, still filled with cookies. "Thank God for Chef Renauld. Her snacks are the only thing easing my stress."

"When I fell off my horse a few years ago, she made me seven different kinds of soup," Jack says, reaching for another cookie. "We're certainly lucky to have her." He bites into it, nodding at the satisfying crunching sound. "But I, for one, am not stressed at all. Because I know the Royal Investigators are on the case."

I watch as Joe shifts in his sleep, his massive paw coming to rest protectively over Luma's smaller form. The collie doesn't seem to mind, snuggling closer into Joe's thick fur. At least someone's finding peace tonight.

"Speaking of investigating… tell me about Ambassador Franklin," I say, drawing my legs up underneath me in the chair. Over my sweatpants, I'm wrapped in one of Jack's hoodie sweatshirts, which hangs off me like a tent but smells comfortingly of him. "Is there anything you left out? Something you didn't want to say in front of Officer Basilier?"

Jack pretends to look shocked. "Are you, Miss Orange, asking me for secrets of state? That's decidedly un-duchess-like of you."

I lean across the table and kiss him gently. "I believe I'm entitled to every secret."

"That you are," he agrees. "Sadly, there are none. The truth is as I said. The Ambassador was a lovely man. Pleasant. Genuinely pleasant, which is rare in diplomatic circles. No hidden agenda, no power plays. Just a decent man trying to do right by his country without steamrolling ours." He sets his cup down with a quiet clink.

"Those kind of people do tend to turn up dead, don't they?" I think out loud. "I hate to see good people harmed. It's the root motivator for my vigilante justice."

"That's why you and I get along so well," he smirks, taking another sip of his drink. "We're both rebels."

I raise an eyebrow at him to communicate that I hardly see him as a rebel. He reads my expression with the ease of someone who has— at this point— seen every look I have to offer.

"I *am!*" He exclaims. "You should have seen the lengths I went to pushing this compromise about the Island of Lilacs through! It's quite a valuable property given its location—"

"So, it's basically a maritime rest stop?"

"Essentially, yes. There's a small harbor, a supply store that's been there for over a century, and more recently, an avian research station studying migratory patterns of several endangered bird species." He leans back in his chair. "Scientifically valuable, economically useful. It was worth fighting over. And you'd be surprised how many diplomats weren't pleased with the compromise. Some of them wanted an all-out war."

"Some of them like…" I push, sensing there's something there.

"Well, come to think of it," Jack admits. "Prime Minister Floridán was rather pushy. He was hoping Monrovia could get sole ownership of the island. He's quite the nationalist. He was mad but—"

"Mad enough to kill!" I exclaim, jumping up with mock theatrics.

Jack laughs and passes me another cookie. "I fear that Officer Basilier will jump to that conclusion when she searches his public statements on the pending compromise. She has quite the history of arresting innocent public figures."

"She's my friend now," I say smugly.

"I noticed that," Jack laughs. "Just don't forget where your true loyalties lie if she gets handsy and throws me in jail again."

"That was *one time*," I tease. "And look at you! You're stronger for it!"

"The fact that she put me in jail, I can forgive," he says

seriously. "But when she locked *you* up? That's something I will never let go." There's a dark look on his face that tells me he's not kidding anymore. "Be her friend, certainly— but know that I have not forgotten."

I wave a hand in the air. "That's water under the bridge! We're working together now. Officer Basilier sees me as a real detective. I wonder if I should give her a nickname. What do you think about Officer B?"

"Love it," Jack agrees, before adding ironically, "She'll be thrilled, I'm sure."

Joe snuffles in his sleep, making that half-growl sound he makes when chasing dream rabbits. Under different circumstances, it would make me smile.

"What happens to the vote now?" I ask.

"It will likely be postponed. Antanaro will need to appoint a new Ambassador, review the agreement again..." He spreads his hands in a gesture of futility. "Months of work, potentially undone in a single night. I'll do all I can to fast track it, though"

I glance around the vast library, its towering shelves suddenly seeming less like guardians of knowledge and more like perfect hiding places for secrets—or people with secrets. "It's strange having the castle so full of strangers," I admit. "I've gotten used to knowing everyone here."

"And now one of them might be a murderer," Jack finishes my thought.

"Exactly." I hug my knees closer to my chest.

"If it helps, this isn't typical for royal weddings," Jack says with a hint of gallows humor. "Usually it's just family drama and wardrobe malfunctions."

"Is it weird that I'd prefer those?" I reach for another cookie, the buttery sweetness a small comfort against the bitterness of our conversation.

Jack reaches across the space between our chairs and takes

my hand. His palm is warm from the teacup, his touch gentle but grounding.

"Enough murder talk for one night," Jack says suddenly, rising from his chair with newfound energy. "We have a wedding to plan, and I refuse to let a diplomatic crisis derail our special day." He moves toward one of the library's far shelves, the one tucked behind the encyclopedias that nobody ever reads. I watch as he reaches up and pulls down a large, leather-bound book that I immediately recognize— our wedding scrapbook, the one Maggie insisted we create to keep all our ideas organized. The sight of it sends a flutter of both excitement and anxiety through my chest.

We haven't been able to agree on anything so far, and if I'm being honest—it makes me feel insecure. "Not this," I say, shaking my head. "The book of disagreement."

"The book of possibility!" Jack says. He returns to his seat, placing the scrapbook on the table between us. " We need something normal to focus on that isn't murder or a diplomatic crisis." He slides the book closer to me. "Besides, if we don't make some decisions soon, Maggie will make them for us. And we both know that will end with you in the world's largest Barbie doll dress."

I grimace at the thought. For all her efficiency and good intentions, Maggie's taste runs decidedly more... *royal* than mine. Last week, she showed me sketches for bridesmaid dresses that looked like whipped cream in a spiral.

"Fair point," I concede, leaning forward to open the scrapbook. The first page is covered with images of white-sand beaches, crystal-clear waters, and palm trees swaying in a gentle breeze. TROPICAL DESTINATION WEDDING is written across the top in Maggie's perfect calligraphy.

Jack points to a particularly stunning photo of a beachfront ceremony at sunset. "What about this? We could fly everyone to a private island. Just imagine saying our vows with our toes in the sand, the sound of waves in the background..."

I wrinkle my nose. "And sand in places where sand should never be? Sand in my wedding dress, sand in the cake, sand in Joe's fur for months afterward?" I shake my head firmly. "Besides, Luma would hate it too. She'd spend the whole time trying to herd the waves."

As if hearing her name, Luma's ears twitch in her sleep, but she doesn't wake. Joe remains equally oblivious, his massive body rising and falling with each breath.

"I suppose you're right," Jack acknowledges with a slight frown. "Though I was rather looking forward to seeing you in a beach wedding dress."

"I don't mind the beach," I say, revealing my *true* worry. "But think about what kind of a message a bunch of private planes send? It makes it seem like we think our wedding is more important than the environment. The emissions alone could harm so many endangered species."

"You're right," Jack agrees seriously. "That idea is out."

He turns the page. The next spread showcases the main royal palace in Monrovia's capital—a structure so grand and imposing it makes Atwood Castle look like a cozy cottage in comparison. Golden spires reach toward the heavens, marble staircases wide enough for twenty people to walk abreast, and ballrooms that could host small countries. TRADITIONAL ROYAL WEDDING AT THE QUEEN'S CASTLE, the caption declares.

My throat tightens at the thought. "This is... a lot."

Jack studies my face carefully. "It would be the traditional *expectation*," he says gently. "Every royal wedding for the past three centuries has taken place there. I know my aunt would be thrilled. It's what the King would have wanted, God rest his soul."

"This was the chosen spot for three centuries of royals who were raised knowing they'd one day be standing on those steps," I point out. "Not former zookeepers who still some-times eat cereal for dinner."

"The Duke and Duchess of Westmoreland had their wedding there just last year," Jack continues. "Two thousand guests, broadcast live to the entire country. It was quite the spectacle." His tone remains neutral, but I can sense he's testing my reaction.

"Two thousand people watching me walk down the aisle?" My voice rises slightly. "Three thousand opportunities to trip, or say the wrong thing, or have my dress malfunction?" I shake my head vehemently. "Jack, I can't do that. All those eyes on me..."

"You handle the animals here with perfect confidence," he points out.

"Animals don't judge your choice of wedding colors or critique your vows on social media," I counter. "Besides, if Joe barks during the ceremony, they'd probably have him removed by the royal guard."

Jack chuckles at that. "You have a point there." He sighs, staring at the page. I can't help but feel it represents some-thing to him— maybe coming full circle from his bachelor days spent on a yacht to becoming a fully functioning member of the royal family. "Perhaps this isn't the one, either," he says gently.

I turn the page again, hoping for a more appealing option. The next spread shows Atwood Castle decorated for a grand celebration— the courtyard transformed with twinkling lights, the great hall filled with guests, and photographers positioned strategically throughout. BIG WEDDING AT ATWOOD, WITH PRESS COVERAGE, reads the heading.

"This seems... slightly less terrifying," I admit cautiously. "At least I know the layout of Atwood. But the press?" I tap one of the photos showing a line of photographers. "Really?"

Jack sighs, running a hand through his hair. "I know it's not ideal, but I'm not sure how to avoid it entirely. As a royal, there's a certain expectation of transparency. The people feel invested in our lives, our milestones."

"*Your* life," I correct him. "I didn't sign up to be a public figure."

"You did when you agreed to marry me," he says softly, and I can tell he's trying to be gentle but firm. "Royal weddings aren't just personal celebrations, they're national events. They give people joy, hope, something positive to focus on in difficult times."

I understand his point, intellectually at least. But the thought of camera flashes and reporters shouting questions makes my palms sweat. "I just... I always pictured something small. Intimate. Just us and the people who really matter to us."

"Like what?" Jack asks, his tone genuinely curious.

I close my eyes, allowing myself to imagine it. "Maybe right here at Atwood, but just in the gardens. A simple ceremony with close friends and family. Joe as the ring bearer. Luma as the flower girl." I open my eyes to find Jack watching me intently. "No press, no thousand-person guest list of people I've never met. Just... us, being real."

"That does sound lovely," he admits. "I don't know how it's possible, given what I am," he motions at himself up and down as if he's Frankenstein's's monster.

We sit in silence for a moment, the crackle of the fire and the soft snoring of our dogs the only sounds in the room. I can see Jack is torn— between tradition and my comfort, between royal duty and personal happiness.

"We'll figure it out," he finally says, but I can tell from his expression that he's as uncertain as I am about how to reconcile our different visions. "There has to be a compromise somewhere."

"There has to be," I say, not entirely convinced. "There always is."

Or at least, there always has *been,* I think. In the past, we've always worked out our differences. What if now, it's too late?

He closes the scrapbook gently. "Let's sleep on it."

As we rise to wake our sleeping dogs, I can't help but wonder if this is what our married life will always be like— a constant negotiation between the life I expected and the royal reality. And in this moment, with a murder to solve and a wedding to plan— the wedding seems more daunting.

Five

IT'S MORNING, and our cozy Royal Investigators office is a safe haven against the overcast October day outside. Joe pads over to his oversized dog bed in the corner— a necessity I insisted on when Maggie and I leased this space— while I dump my bag on the desk and take in the sight of my business partner already hard at work. Maggie has been here for hours, judging by the empty coffee cups and the meticulous crime board she's assembling on the far wall. She's already decorated our office for Halloween, meticulously placing olive-branch-and-twinkle garlands across the desks. Two pumpkins sit in the corner, and a cackling witch stands by the door to welcome visitors.

I glance at our corkboard, noticing that Maggie has already set up information for our next case. Five faces stare back at me from a collection of hastily printed photographs, all connected by yellow threads to a central image— Ambassador Franklin, looking far more alive than when I last saw him sprawled across the castle ballroom floor.

"You started without me," I say, reaching for the extra coffee Maggie always brings. It's lukewarm now, but caffeine is caffeine, and after last night's late conversation with Jack, I need all the help I can get.

"Couldn't sleep," Maggie replies without turning around. She's wearing her practical clothes today— tailored slacks and a crisp blouse— a far cry from her ornate costume last night. "I keep seeing his face. The Ambassador's, I mean."

"I know what you mean," I murmur, taking a sip of coffee and grimacing at both the temperature and the memory. "Every time I closed my eyes last night, I saw him lying there."

Joe settles into his bed with a dramatic sigh, clearly disappointed that we're discussing murder instead of providing him with treats. His massive head rests on his paws, but his eyes remain alert, watching us with that peculiar intelligence that sometimes makes me wonder if he understands more than he lets on.

"So," I say, approaching the board and standing beside Maggie, "what have we got?"

Maggie steps back, gesturing to her handiwork with a flourish. Our crime board has transformed overnight from a simple corkboard where we post community notices to a proper detective's wall of suspicion. In the center is a photo of Ambassador Franklin—not the death scene, thankfully, but an official portrait showing him in diplomatic regalia, smiling benignly at the camera.

"Ambassador Franklin," Maggie says, tapping his photo. "Fifty-three years old, career diplomat, served as Antanaro's Ambassador to Monrovia for twelve years. Well-respected, no known enemies, generally considered a moderate voice in Antanaran politics."

"And now dead on our watch," I add grimly.

"Which brings us to our suspects," Maggie says, pointing to the five photographs arranged in a semi-circle around Franklin's image. Yellow threads connect each to the central photo, a visual representation of the literal thread of evidence found in the Ambassador's hand.

I move closer, studying each face in turn. "Suspect number one: Missy Adeline, Antanaran movie star and national treasure." The photo shows her at some red-carpet event, looking flawless in a form-fitting gown, her smile dazzling for the cameras.

"Thirty-six years old, known for her dramatic roles and equally dramatic off-screen activism," Maggie reads from her notes. "Deeply nationalistic about Antanaro. Her publicist, Sacks, arranged for her to wear a gown made from that yellow fabric by Ms. Labelle for last night's ball."

"Motive?" I ask, taking another sip of my disappointing coffee.

"That's where it gets interesting," Maggie says, her eyes lighting up with that particular gleam she gets when she's puzzling through a mystery. "According to my sources, Missy is very much a patriot. She's involved in multiple pro-nationalist causes for her country."

"So she might have wanted Franklin dead to derail the vote," I muse, studying Missy's perfect features. "But would a movie star really commit murder over an island dispute?"

"People have killed for less," Maggie points out. "And she wouldn't be the first celebrity with extreme political views."

I move to the next photo— it's of Sacks. He looks just as slick in the picture as he did in real life. His paisley shirt in the photo makes me wince, remembering the eyesore he wore to the ball. Paisley shirts seem to be a favorite of his.

"Suspect number two: Sacks, Missy's publicist and fashion victim. He's been with Missy for six years," Maggie continues. "Managed her transition from rom-com darling to serious dramatic actress. Known for being ruthlessly protective of her image and career."

"Would he kill to protect her reputation?" I wonder aloud.

"Probably," Maggie shrugs. "His wagon is hitched to hers.

She's his biggest client. But I can't see how her reputation would be connected to the Ambassador. They're from two totally different worlds."

Joe makes a snuffling sound from his bed, almost as if offering his own opinion on the matter. I glance over at him. "What do you think, Joe? Is Sacks our killer?"

Joe's tail thumps once against his bed—not exactly a ringing endorsement of our theory.

Moving on, I study the third photo— it's of Ms. Labelle, the dressmaker. The picture is accompanied by a newspaper article about her opening *Maison Labelle*. It outlines her rise from poverty to successful dressmaker. "Suspect number three: Ms. Labelle, the dressmaker."

"Thirty-four years old, self-made businesswoman who opened her boutique in the village three years ago," Maggie recites. "Born poor in rural Monrovia, worked her way up through the fashion industry. Her shop, *Maison Labelle*, can make more than just dresses now. Suits. Custom shirts."

"And she's the source of our murder fabric," I note, tapping the yellow material connecting her to Franklin. "She made something for each suspect using that specific material."

"Including herself," Maggie points out. "That clutch she was carrying last night? Same yellow sequined fabric."

I frown, trying to remember my brief interaction with Ms. Labelle during last night's questioning. "She seemed genuinely shocked when she saw the fabric sample. Almost afraid."

"Maybe because she realized it implicated her as much as anyone else," Maggie suggests.

"Or maybe because she knows exactly which one of her clients could be behind this, and that knowledge scares her," I counter. "She might have overheard something at a fitting. We should start with her. She's the common thread— literally— between all our suspects."

Maggie nods in agreement before moving on to the fourth photo of Prime Minister Floridán leading a session of parliament. "That brings us to our most dangerous suspect number four: Prime Minister Floridán."

"Now there's a man who looks like he enjoys firing people," I observe.

"Forty-nine years old, elected Prime Minister of Monrovia three years ago on a nationalist platform," Maggie explains. "He represents the new government, as opposed to the traditional liberal world order. He likes to have complete authority and is... less than supportive of the royal family."

"Jack mentioned him," I recall. "Said he's a real treat."

"That's putting it mildly," Maggie says with a grimace. "He's publicly stated that the monarchy is an outdated institution that drains resources from 'real Monrovians.'"

"And the island vote?"

"He's against the compromise. No surprise there. But I can't *imagine* he'd kill for it. If the Prime Minister wanted someone dead, he'd never do it himself. Why dirty his own hands, right?"

"Good point," I agree moving to the final photo of the Prime Minister's wife, Geneviève Floridán. Her intelligent eyes look at me from the still, which looks to have been taken from a magazine. "That leaves suspect number five: Geneviève Floridán, the Prime Minister's wife."

"Forty-three years old. She's actually a brilliant legal mind," Maggie says with noticeable respect in her voice. "She was her husband's campaign strategist and is widely credited with his electoral success. Works behind the scenes, but those in political circles say she's the real brains of the operation."

"The power behind the throne," I muse.

"Exactly," Maggie agrees. "But again, I can't see why she would want Ambassador Franklin dead."

I step back, taking in the full board with all five suspects. "So we have a nationalistic movie star, her ambitious publicist, a dressmaker with connections to everyone, a Prime Minister who hates the monarchy, and his legally-savvy wife. All wearing something made from the same yellow fabric."

"And all with access to him at the ball last night," Maggie adds.

Joe rises from his bed and stretches, his massive body extending to its full impressive length before he pads over to join us at the board. He sits between us, his intelligent eyes scanning the photos as if he, too, is evaluating the suspects.

"There's something else," Maggie says hesitantly, reaching out to touch Ambassador Franklin's photo. "Have you noticed... I mean, it's probably nothing, but..."

"What?" I prompt when she trails off.

"The Ambassador," she says, glancing at me. "He looks a bit like Jack, doesn't he?"

"He does," I agree, leaning in to look at the picture. "When I first saw his body I thought it *was* Jack." My hands tremble at the memory. "I thought the worst and then when it wasn't him, I feel awful saying it, but… I was relieved."

I lean closer, studying Franklin's features more carefully. The salt-and-pepper hair, the distinguished jawline, the similar build and height... There is a resemblance. Not identical, but enough that someone might mistake one for the other in dim lighting, especially with masks involved.

"Everyone was wearing masks," Maggie finishes my thought. "Rebecca, it's just a theory, but what if…"

We look at each other, the same disturbing possibility forming in both our minds.

"You don't think..." I start.

"I hope not," Maggie says, her voice barely above a whisper. "But just in case, tell Jack to be careful. The killer is still in the castle. And if they missed the first time…"

"They might try again," I nod.

The implication settles over us like a heavy blanket.

Joe nudges my hand with his nose, pulling me back from

the edge of panic. I scratch behind his ears automatically, the familiar gesture helping to ground me.

"We need to consider every possibility," I say, forcing my voice to remain steady. "But let's focus on what we know for sure. The fabric evidence points to one of these five people. And Ms. Labelle is the one who made all the items."

"So we start with her," Maggie agrees, already reaching for her tablet to make notes. We should also ask everybody where they were when the lights went out just before the murder happened. If we can place them around the room, we can try to figure out who had time to get to the Ambassador."

"Great idea!" I say, nodding. "Let's head to Ms. Labelle's shop. And maybe, let's grab a proper coffee at *Le Petit Scone* on the way," I say, holding up my now-cold cup with a grimace. "Henri has seasonal pumpkin-cinnamon lattes on the menu."

"And maybe something for Joe?" Maggie suggests with a smile, looking down at the massive dog who's now sitting at attention, clearly recognizing that his name, said with such affection, usually means treats are forthcoming.

"It's only right," I agree. "He's part of the investigating team, after all."

As Maggie gathers her tablet and I collect my bag, I take one last look at the board. Five suspects, one victim, and yellow material connecting them all. Somewhere in this tangle is a killer— a killer who's still living in Castle Atwood, my favorite place in the world. The place I call home.

Whoever did this better watch out, I think. *Because I'm not going to rest until I find them.*

CHAPTER
Six

MAISON LABELLE SITS like a pristine jewel among the weathered stone buildings of Atwood Village, its freshly painted pastel blue exterior standing out against the faded charm of the neighborhood. I pause on the sidewalk, Joe's leash wrapped around my wrist, and take in the elegant cursive lettering above the door that announces we've arrived at our destination. I take a sip of the pumpkin-cinnamon latte I've just picked up from *Le Petit Scone*, sighing as the warm brew trickles through my system. Through *Maison Labelle's* gleaming front window, a Halloween-themed display promises seasonal fashions: an orange trench-coat; a star-studded t-shirt; a pair of jeans with pumpkins embroidered up the thigh. It's all one-of-a-kind couture. The entire setup screams *"exclusive boutique where someone like me would normally never shop."*

"Ready?" Maggie asks, her tablet already tucked under her arm for notetaking. In her other hand, she balances a caramel-apple tea, also compliments of Henri at *Le Petit Scone.*

"As I'll ever be," I reply, giving Joe's leash a gentle tug. "Remember, Joe, best behavior. No drooling on the expensive fabrics."

Joe looks up at me with an expression that somehow manages to be both offended and amused. Two hundred and fifty pounds of Tibetan Mastiff have never looked more dignified.

The bell above the door chimes delicately as we enter, announcing our arrival into a space that feels more like a museum than a shop. The scent of new fabric fills the air, and overhead chandeliers illuminate what can only be described as a temple to fashion. Every surface gleams— polished wooden floors, sparkling glass display cases, and chrome racks that hold garments arranged by color with military precision.

"Wow," I whisper to Maggie. "I feel like I should have showered twice this morning."

She smiles knowingly. "Ms. Labelle is famous for her attention to detail."

That's an understatement. The shop is immaculate in a way that makes me suddenly conscious of every dog hair clinging to my pants. Joe seems to sense this too, sitting down primly beside me as if trying to minimize his considerable footprint in this shrine to elegance.

"Good morning," a melodic voice calls from the back of the shop. Ms. Labelle emerges from behind a beaded curtain, looking far more composed than she did during last night's questioning. Her asymmetrical black dress is clearly her own design, tailored to perfection, and her clever eyes quickly assess us— an odd trio of investigators invading her pristine domain.

"Ms. Orange, Ms. Lefevere," she nods to each of us, then her gaze drops to Joe. "And... Joe, was it? Welcome to *Maison Labelle*."

"Thank you for seeing us," Maggie says, stepping forward with her usual diplomatic grace. "We know this must be a difficult day after all that's happened."

Ms. Labelle's smile doesn't quite reach her eyes. "Yes,

well... one must carry on, mustn't one?" She gestures toward the back of the shop. "Please, follow me. Bring your drinks with you, of course."

We follow her through the beaded curtain into a small but equally immaculate workspace. A cutting table dominates the center, surrounded by dress forms in various states of creation. Bolts of fabric line the walls, organized by type and color in a way that makes my apartment's "clean enough" standard seem positively slovenly. In one corner, a small seating area with a vintage settee and two chairs surrounds a tea service that looks ready for a royal visit.

"Please, sit," Ms. Labelle offers, and I guide Joe to a spot beside the settee where he can observe without knocking anything over with his tail. He settles with a soft huff, his eyes never leaving Ms. Labelle. "Help yourself if you'd like tea," she adds, nodding at the tea station in the corner.

"This is quite the operation you have," I say earnestly. "How long have you been in business?"

"Three years in this location," she replies, passing a plate of scones. "Though I've been making clothes since I was a child."

"It shows," Maggie compliments, glancing around. "Your work is extraordinary."

Ms. Labelle's posture relaxes at the praise. "Thank you. I've worked hard to build this place." Her eyes drift around the workspace with unmistakable pride. "It's everything to me."

"We'd like to talk to you again about all of the suspects from last night," I say, deciding to skip the small talk. "Now that it's just us, we can be more— honest with each other."

Ms. Labelle offers a slight nod, which is enough to make me keep talking. "Let's start with Prime Minister Floridán. You dressed him for the evening. What was his demeanor when he came in for the fitting?"

The shift in her presence is subtle but immediate— a slight

stiffening of her shoulders, a momentary pause before she takes a deliberate sip of tea.

"He came in about two weeks ago with his wife," she confirms. "Ginevière wanted a dress that was patriotic, and she thought her husband needed something to match. She's quite the brains of the operation, isn't she?"

I lean in, sensing that Ms. Labelle would like to say more. "Ms. Labelle, I hate to ask this because I understand it's the first code of customer service not to report on your clients. Maggie and I—in addition to being Royal Investigators— both serve as staff at the castle, so we understand what it means to be loyal to those you serve."

"I know," Ms. Labelle nods, setting down her teacup. "I saw in the magazines you are the castle animal trainer. And now, soon to be a duchess."

"Yes," I confirm, thinking to myself: *If Jack and I can ever agree on a wedding.* But I push the thought away and focus on the investigation in front of me. "That's why I understand loyalty. But a man was killed, and if there's anything you heard from the Prime Minister or his wife, you can tell us. We won't let him know it was you."

Tears start to pool in Ms. Labelle's eyes, but she doesn't let them fall. Instead, she takes a deep, steadying breath and leans in. "There *was* something. During the fitting."

I'm afraid to breathe in case I scare her away. Maggie and I exchange a glance. Even Joe sits rigid on the floor, afraid to move. We act as if a butterfly has landed on us. In the silence, Ms. Labelle finds her voice.

"The Prime Minister was talking about the Ambassador," Ms. Labelle continues. "He told his wife they had to stay away from Ambassador Franklin at the masquerade. She was urging him to 'be the bigger man.' To go and say hello. She told him it would be a smart political move. But Prime Minister Floridán wanted nothing to do with it. He said the man was disgusting and he would not agree to say hello."

Maggie and I lean in, waiting.

"And?" Maggie says, sensing there's more to the story.

"And—" Ms. Labelle nods, picking up her teacup again. "I have it on good authority from one of my own high-profile clients that the Prime Minister's wife, Geneviève, used to date Ambassador Franklin, long before she was married."

Maggie gasps, almost dropping her cup. Joe shifts position, letting out an audible sigh.

"Are you sure?" I ask, intrigued by this new possible motivation.

"Yes," Ms. Labelle says, throwing her hands in the air and looking suddenly worried. "But you did not hear it from me. If you say I told you, I'll deny it."

"Can we see the fabric?" Maggie asks. "The one found in the Ambassador's hand. It just seems strange that so many powerful people happened to pick the same thing..."

Ms. Labelle sets down her teacup with a soft clink. "Follow me," she says, rising gracefully.

She leads us back into the main shop area, stopping before a rack of fabric samples near the front window. Her fingers dance across the various textures and colors before pulling out a small square of brilliant yellow material studded with gold sequins that catch the light with every movement.

"This is it," she says, holding it up. "Or rather, this is a sample of it. I ordered this specific sequined material from Paris for a special collection. It's quite distinctive—a particular shade of yellow with these unique gold sequins that catch the light differently depending on the angle." Her description matches almost word for word what she told us last night.

"It's beautiful," Maggie comments, reaching out to touch the sample. "Now that I see it in its raw form like this, I understand why so many customers chose it. It's almost the exact shade on the Monrovian flag."

"It's hard to find. A limited edition," Ms. Labelle explains, handling the fabric with reverence. "The manufacturer only produced a small quantity. I purchased nearly all of it—at considerable expense, I might add."

"And you made only five items from this fabric?" I clarify.

She nods, returning the sample to its place on the rack. "Yes. Missy Adeline's enormous ballgown, which was the largest piece. Sacks' shirt accents and socks. Prime Minister Floridán's tie. His wife's tasteful dress," she hesitates, then adds, "And my own clutch."

"And the fabric was particularly expensive?" Maggie asks, tapping notes into her tablet.

"Very," Ms. Labelle confirms, leading us back to the tea area. "In fact, it was a risk for me to purchase it at all. The shop has been... struggling." The admission clearly costs her, her voice dropping as if sharing a shameful secret.

"Struggling?" I prompt gently.

She sinks back onto her chair, shoulders dropping slightly. "The last year has been difficult. Luxury items are always the first to go when people tighten their belts."

Maggie and I exchange glances. Financial trouble is always a compelling motive.

"But the Royal Masquerade brought so much business!" Ms. Labelle's face brightens. "I owe you a thank you, Rebecca Orange. Your wedding has changed my life for the better."

And ended Ambassador Franklin's, I think, feeling pained.

"The announcement of the masquerade was a godsend," Ms. Labelle continues. "Suddenly everyone needed formal wear, costumes, masks. I've been working sixteen-hour days for weeks." She gestures toward the half-finished gowns on the dress forms. "And now..."

"Now?" I echo.

"Well..." A hint of color touches her cheeks. "Since the... incident... business has actually increased. The press has been calling non-stop since word leaked about the material being found on the Ambassador. Everyone wants to know about the 'murder fabric' and who was wearing it."

"And how do you feel about that?" I ask, watching her closely.

"Terrible about the circumstances, of course," she says quickly—too quickly. "Ambassador Franklin seemed like a kind man. But..." She hesitates.

"But?" Maggie prompts.

"But I can't deny the publicity has been good for business." She looks genuinely conflicted, torn between shame at benefiting from tragedy and relief at her shop's improved fortunes. "Just yesterday, I received three orders from people who specifically requested items made from the same yellow fabric. As if it's some kind of... macabre souvenir."

"Did you have enough left to fill those orders?" I ask, curious.

"No," she says, shaking her head. "After the masks and the items for the ball, there was nothing left. But I've ordered more— a different shade, but similar enough to satisfy the morbid curiosity." Her fingers twist in her lap. "It's distasteful, but I have a business to run."

Joe has inched closer to Ms. Labelle during our conversation, his massive head now near her knee. She notices suddenly and flinches slightly.

"He won't hurt you," I assure her. "He's just curious."

"He's... very large," she observes nervously.

"Ms. Labelle," I say gently. "Where were you when the lights went out the night of the murder? Where in the room, I mean?"

Ms. Labelle shifts her weight from side to side, looking anxious. "I was— why, I was talking with one of my customers." Her expression is strained, as if she's trying to remember. "I was by the dessert table. Why on earth would you ask such a thing?"

The sudden shift in her demeanor is interesting. I glance at Maggie, who gives me a subtle nod.

"I think we have what we need for now," I say, rising to my feet. "Thank you for your time, Ms. Labelle. We may need to follow up with additional questions."

"Of course," she says, relief evident in her voice as she begins ushering us toward the door. "Anything to help find who did this terrible thing."

As we step back onto the village street, the bell chiming our departure, Joe gives himself a vigorous shake as if trying to dispel the boutique's pristine atmosphere from his fur.

"Well, that was illuminating," Maggie says once we're out of earshot.

"Wasn't it?" I reply, processing what we've learned. "The Prime Minister's wife used to date the Ambassador? How did we not know this?"

"I can ask around the castle," Maggie assures me. "If it's true, someone will be able to verify the rumor. And how about Ms. Labelle's financial troubles? She wasn't a top suspect in my mind, but now... Rebecca, she might have motivation."

Maggie, Joe, and I continue down the cobblestone street, turning the corner toward the village square. The familiar green awning of what used to be Rodrigo's newsstand comes into view. After Rodrigo's murder last year, his protégé Zacharia took over the business, maintaining its reputation as the village's primary source for newspapers, magazines, and gossip.

"I don't know," I say, shaking my head at Maggie. "I just can't picture Ms. Labelle killing for fame. I doubt her story is getting that much attention anyway."

As we approach the newsstand, my steps slow involuntarily. The front display rack is dominated by magazines and tabloids, all featuring variations of the same headline: "DEADLY FASHION: MURDER FABRIC TRACED TO

LOCAL DESIGNER." Several show photographs of *Maison Labelle's* storefront, and one particularly sensational cover features a crude mock-up of a hand clutching yellow material, droplets of red artfully splattered across the image.

Maggie gives me a meaningful look. "You were saying?"

"Oh, hell," I mutter, stopping to stare at the display. "No wonder she's getting calls from the press. This is..."

"Exactly the kind of publicity you can't buy," Maggie finishes, her expression troubled.

Joe sniffs at the newsstand, then looks up at me with those wise eyes that sometimes seem to understand more than any dog should.

"You're thinking what I'm thinking, aren't you?" I ask Maggie, keeping my voice low as Zacharia watches us curiously from behind his counter.

"Absolutely," Maggie says. "And I'm thinking about it with more judgement, because I'm meaner than you."

I think about the pride in Ms. Labelle's eyes as she looked around her shop, the reverence with which she handled her fabrics, the way she described the place as "everything to me."

"People have killed to protect less," I say finally.

"We need to look deeper into her finances," Maggie decides, making a note on her tablet. "And find out exactly how much this publicity has improved her business."

We turn away from the newsstand, continuing toward our next destination. Joe walks between us, his presence reassuring as we navigate the increasingly complex threads of this investigation. One thing is becoming clear: in a case where everyone is connected by a distinctive yellow material, the artist who wielded the material for her creations might be the most suspicious thread of all.

CHAPTER

Seven

CAFÉ DE FLORE sits like a flowery oasis in the middle of the village, its green-and-white striped awning fluttering beneath the October wind. Two bales of hay frame the entrance, pots of orange flowers stacked on top. *Leave it to Jocelyn to have the cutest Halloween decorations already in place.*

I pause outside, adjusting Joe's collar—a completely unnecessary gesture since my massive dog always looks more put-together than I do— and glance at Maggie, who's checking her watch with the precision of someone who considers being on time as being late.

"Two minutes to spare," she announces, tapping her tablet to sleep mode. "Officer Basilier is already inside, back corner table. She's been there for twenty minutes."

"Of course she has," I sigh, pushing open the door. The sweet scent of honey and lavender envelops us immediately, along with the gentle hum of morning conversation. "Does she think punctuality is a competitive sport?"

"Knowing Basilier? Probably. Remember, no dog jokes, no sarcasm about her uniform, and no mentioning what she looked like in a ballgown."

"I would never," I protest, though all three were definitely on my mental list of icebreakers. Joe huffs beside me, as if he too has been instructed to be on his best behavior. His massive paws click softly against the polished wooden floor as we weave through the café.

Officer Basilier sits at a table beneath a fall-themed garland, her back to the wall, eyes scanning the room with practiced vigilance. She's dressed in civilian clothes— dark jeans and a crisp button-down shirt— but she still radiates authority like it's a cologne she can't wash off. Her hair, usually pulled back in a severe bun, falls loosely around her shoulders, making her look almost approachable. Almost.

"Orange. Lefevere." She nods at each of us in turn, then her eyes drop to Joe. "And the furry detective. Right on time."

"We aim to please," I say, sliding into the seat across from her while Joe arranges his substantial bulk beneath the table. His head emerges between Maggie and me, like a furry submarine periscope.

Before we can launch into police business, Jocelyn glides over to our table, a gentle smile on her face and a notepad in hand. The café owner's quiet demeanor belies her keen observation skills—a trait I've come to appreciate during our previous visits.

"Good morning, ladies," she says softly, her voice barely rising above the ambient café chatter. "The usual for you, Rebecca? And Maggie, would you like to try our new pumpkin spice chai tea? It's perfect for this weather."

"Actually," Officer Basilier interjects, "we'll all have the cinnamon tea. And whatever pastry has pumpkin in it." She glances at me. "Orange mentioned you have the best seasonal treats."

I blink in surprise. I *did* mention that to Officer Basilier, but it was weeks ago, during a completely unrelated conversation about why I liked this café. The fact that she remembered catches me off guard.

She likes me more than she lets on, I think to myself smiling.

Way to go, Rebecca Orange. Making friends out of even the prickliest of people.

"And something for your handsome companion?" Jocelyn asks, bending slightly to make eye contact with Joe, who responds with his most dignified expression.

"He'd love one of your special dog biscuits," I reply. "The ones with the peanut butter center, if you have them."

Jocelyn nods, her eyes crinkling at the corners. "Always for Joe. I'll be right back with your order."

As she moves away, Officer Basilier leans forward, all business now. "So. Ms. Labelle's shop. What did you learn?"

Maggie opens her tablet, ever-prepared. "She confirmed making items from the yellow and gold sequined material for all five suspects, including a small clutch for herself."

"And she's in financial trouble," I add. "Or *was*, until a murder conveniently connected to the distinctive fabric made her shop the talk of the town."

Officer Basilier nods thoughtfully. "Motive, opportunity, and now her business is booming. What about means? Any sense she'd be physically capable of stabbing the Ambassador?"

I think back to Ms. Labelle's slender frame, her manicured hands that handled fabric with such precision. "She's stronger than she looks," I say slowly. "You can see it in her forearms—years of cutting fabric, operating industrial sewing machines. And stabbing doesn't always require brute strength, just determination."

"And the Ambassador wasn't a large man," Maggie points out. "Plus, in a crowded ballroom, with the element of surprise..."

Our conversation pauses as Jocelyn returns with a tray bearing three steaming cinnamon teas, each topped with a delicate foam design of a different flower. She sets a plate of pastries in the center of the table—golden, flaky things drizzled with honey and dotted with what look like crystallized pumpkin candies. Joe's treat, an oversized bone-shaped biscuit, she places directly on the floor beside him with a gentle pat to his head.

"Enjoy, ladies," she says with that same soft smile before drifting back to the counter. "And gentledog."

Joe doesn't wait for permission, his massive jaws making short work of the biscuit while still managing to look dignified. I watch as Officer Basilier's eyes follow him, a hint of something like envy crossing her face.

"I should get a dog," she says suddenly, taking a sip of her tea. "A big one like Joe. Maybe then I'd get special treatment at cafés too."

"You'd get a dog just to compete with Joe for free biscuits?" I ask, amused.

"No," she replies with surprising sincerity. "I'd get one because... well, look at him. Loyal, protective, good at reading people." She gestures toward Joe, who has finished his treat and now rests his massive head on my lap, his eyes half-closed in contentment. "Plus, unlike most of my colleagues, he doesn't ask stupid questions or contaminate crime scenes."

Maggie and I exchange surprised glances at this rare moment of vulnerability from Officer Basilier. It's easy to forget sometimes that beneath her tough exterior is just a regular person, possibly even one who gets lonely.

"Joe would be happy to share his biscuit sources," I offer, scratching behind his ears. "Though fair warning— once you have a dog, you'll never use the bathroom alone again."

Officer Basilier almost smiles at that, then clears her throat and steers us back to business. "About Ms. Labelle's shop. The publicity boom after the murder— how did that information get out so quickly?"

I take a bite of the pastry, momentarily distracted by how the pumpkin candies and spices combine to create something that tastes like October. "Mm, this is incredible," I mumble, then collect myself. "Sorry. The leak— we're not sure. But by the time we left her shop, the newsstand was already displaying tabloids with headlines about the 'murder fabric' being traced to her."

"Zacharia must have gotten the scoop somehow," Maggie adds, referring to the village's primary purveyor of news and gossip.

Officer Basilier shakes her head, a grimace pulling at her features. "It's impossible to control information these days. One officer makes an offhand comment, one staff member overhears something— next thing you know, it's front-page news with dramatic recreations." She takes a long sip of her tea, leaving a slight foam mustache that she quickly wipes away. "In my day, we could keep things quiet long enough to actually investigate."

"Your day?" I can't help but tease. "How old are you, exactly? Because you're talking like you carried a billy club and wore one of those tall hats."

She narrows her eyes at me, but there's no real heat behind it. "I'm thirty-eight, Orange. And when I started on the force, we didn't have social media turning every local incident into international entertainment."

"Fair point," I concede. "And the publicity does complicate things. If Ms. Labelle is our killer, she's certainly benefiting from her crime."

"Speaking of publicity," Officer Basilier says, reaching into her bag and pulling out a manila folder, "that brings me to why I asked to meet you here instead of the station."

She slides the folder across the table. Maggie, always quicker on the uptake than me, flips it open to reveal two glossy press badges attached to lanyards. Each badge features the title *Jules et Jim* in elaborate script across the top, with the words "PRESS ACCESS" printed beneath in bold lettering.

"What are these for?" I ask, picking one up to examine it closer.

Officer Basilier's mouth curls into what might generously

be called a smile. "I spoke to Zacharia at the newsstand this morning. Turns out, two of our other suspects— Missy Adeline and her publicist, Sacks— will be at a premiere for her new film *Jules et Jim* in the city tomorrow night." She taps the badges. "These get you entry as press. Courtesy of the Monrovian Police Department's relationship with the film board."

I frown, setting the badge back down. "But I thought all the suspects were supposed to stay in town! Why does Missy get to leave?"

"Because she's a movie star," Officer Basilier states flatly, as if explaining a fundamental law of physics. "And movie stars get special treatment." At my deepening frown, she adds, "The Captain approved it since it's only an hour away from Atwood. But she must return immediately after the event."

"So we're supposed to, what— pretend to be entertainment reporters?" I ask, already imagining the disaster of me attempting to talk intelligently about cinema to people who actually know what they're doing.

"You won't need to say much," Officer Basilier assures me. "These badges get you onto the red carpet and into the reception afterward. Your job is to observe Missy and Sacks, see how they interact with others, and listen for anything relevant to our case."

"And if they recognize us?" Maggie asks practically. "We did just interrogate them yesterday."

"Tell them Rebecca is there writing a special column for Zacharia. He's done enough stories on *you*— tell them he gave you your own corner in the magazine to write about anything you want, and you chose to come see this movie."

Having my own column in the tabloid doesn't sound like a bad idea, I think. *Maybe I could tell my side of the story for once.*

Officer Basilier turns to Maggie, "And tell them she brought you, Maggie, as her plus one. That's why I'm sending you two well-meaning amateurs instead of me. You have a plausible reason to be there. Royal connections and all. Rebecca's a public figure now. She'll fit right in."

Joe shifts beneath the table, his tail thumping against my leg as if voting in favor of this undercover mission. I scratch his ear absently, considering the plan.

"We won't exactly blend in with the entertainment press," I point out. "I know nothing about films, and Maggie's idea of cinema is historical documentaries about royal genealogy."

"Hey!" Maggie protests, then concedes with a shrug. "That's fair."

"You don't need to blend in perfectly," Officer Basilier says. "Just enough to observe without raising suspicions. And if you're worried about Joe being too recognizable..." She smiles, then reaches into her bag again and pulls out what appears to be a small vest. "Police K-9 Service Dog identification. For the night, he's officially working with the security team."

I take the vest, oddly touched by how thoroughly she's thought this through. "You really want us on this, don't you?"

Officer Basilier sits back, cupping her tea in both hands. "Look, I've got five suspects, a dead Ambassador, and a political situation that could explode in our faces any moment. I need every advantage I can get." She glances at Joe, then back to me. "And like it or not, Orange, you and your team have a knack for getting people to talk."

"My team?" I repeat, surprised by the term.

She gestures to encompass Maggie, Joe, and me. "The Royal Investigators. Isn't that what you call yourselves? Clearly I've learned I can't beat you, so I've joined you. I thought that was obvious after our last case."

Maggie's face lights up with barely contained excitement. "We'll need background on *Jules et Jim*," she says, already tapping notes into her tablet. "Release date, plot summary, critical reception—enough to sound knowledgeable if questioned."

"And formal wear," I add with a grimace. "I assume we

can't show up in jeans and a dog collar." I glance down at Joe, who somehow manages to look offended at the suggestion he'd wear anything but his finest attire to a film premiere.

"I'll have files sent to your office with everything you need to know about the film," Officer Basilier promises. "As for wardrobe..." She gives me a critical once-over. "I'm sure the Duke can help with that."

The reminder of Jack sends a pang through me. Between investigating Ms. Labelle this morning and now planning for tomorrow's undercover operation, I've barely had time to check in with him. And if our suspicion is correct—that the Ambassador was killed because he resembled Jack—then there's the unsettling possibility that the real target is still in danger.

"One more thing," I say, my voice more serious now. "Have you considered the possibility that Ambassador Franklin wasn't the intended victim? The resemblance between him and Jack, especially with masks involved..."

Officer Basilier nods grimly. "It's on our radar. We've increased security at the castle, and the Duke has been advised to limit public appearances until we resolve this." She hesitates, then adds, "But keep that theory to yourselves for now. If word gets out that the Duke might have been the target, we'll have an even bigger media circus on our hands."

"Understood," Maggie says, always the professional.

I finish my tea, savoring the last hints of cinnamon. "So, tomorrow night—film premiere, fancy clothes, press badges, and a police dog." I reach down to pat Joe's substantial head. "Anything else we should know?"

"Yes," Officer Basilier says, her expression deadly serious. "Don't try to make an arrest on your own, don't reveal you're working with the police, and for God's sake, Orange— don't let that mountain of fur eat the hors d'oeuvres at the reception. I had to call in serious favors for those badges and the vest."

"Joe is a professional," I say with mock indignation. "He would never compromise an investigation for finger food." Below the table, Joe makes a small whining sound that undermines my defense entirely.

Now that we're all in agreement, we clean up our table so as not to leave Jocelyn with any dirty dishes. Then, Maggie, Joe, and I head toward the edge of the village, waving goodbye to Officer Basilier as we start the short walk back to the castle.

Tomorrow night, we become entertainment reporters. Today, we need to learn everything we can about French cinema and how to look like we belong on a red carpet. I glance down at Joe, who stares back with those intelligent eyes that somehow always seem to say exactly what I'm thinking.

"I know, buddy," I murmur as we step back onto the village street. "We're way out of our depth. But when has that ever stopped us before?"

CHAPTER
Eight

I TUG at the hemline of my long black dress for the fifth time in as many minutes, feeling like an impostor in someone else's wardrobe. The fabric falls in elegant lines that somehow make me look taller and more sophisticated than I feel, but all I can think about is how much easier it would be to chase a runaway giraffe in my usual khakis and sensible shoes. Still, undercover work requires sacrifices, and tonight, comfort is mine.

"If you keep fidgeting with that dress, you'll wear a hole in it before we even get to the premiere," Jack says, his eyes crinkling with amusement as we stand outside the castle's main entrance. The evening air carries a slight chill, and the setting sun casts long shadows across the immaculate driveway where we're waiting for Enrique.

"I'm not fidgeting, I'm tactically adjusting," I correct him. "This is what spies do."

"Ah yes, the famous spy technique of constantly drawing attention to one's outfit," Maggie chimes in. Unlike me, she looks completely at home in her midnight blue cocktail dress, as if she attends film premieres every weekend. Her tablet—

ever-present— is tucked into a sleek clutch that matches her outfit perfectly.

Joe sits at my feet, his massive form unusually subdued, as if he senses something important is happening. Luma circles around him, her collie energy in stark contrast to Joe's dignified stillness. She nuzzles against his side, then looks up at Jack with those adoring eyes that seem to say, "Why is everyone dressed so strangely tonight?"

"Are you sure you'll be okay with both of them?" I ask Jack, reaching down to scratch behind Joe's ears. Despite Officer Basilier's generous offer of the K-9 police vest, I've decided to leave Joe home tonight because—very unprofessionally— he found his way into a jar of cookies left out for staff and helped himself to the treats. He's been sick every hour since. Luckily, the cookies didn't have any ingredients that were toxic to dogs—just loads of sugar and butter— but Joe is still paying for the decision. "Joe can get anxious when I'm gone too long, especially when his tummy is upset."

Joe whines and rolls over as if to say I regret every decision I've ever made. I bend down and scratch his stomach. "See, buddy," I say, "We can't be super-detectives if we make ourselves sick eating things we're not supposed to, right?" He licks my hand in agreement.

"We'll be fine," Jack assures me, bending down to pet both dogs. "Won't we, team? We've got a schedule— first, a dignified walk around the east gardens, followed by a nap for Joe, then perhaps a documentary on migratory birds."

"Sounds thrilling," I laugh. "Joe prefers action movies, just so you know. Anything with explosions."

"Of course he does," Jack replies with mock seriousness. "I should have guessed from his sophisticated taste in literature." This is an ongoing joke between us since Jack found Joe sleeping on his first-edition Hemingway last month.

Joe looks between us, his expression somehow conveying

that he understands he's being discussed and doesn't entirely appreciate the humor at his expense.

"I'm sorry you can't come, buddy," I tell him, kneeling down despite the dress's protest. "But I saved your special police vest. We'll use it soon, I promise."

"About that," Jack says, his voice shifting to a more serious tone as I stand back up. "I know Officer Basilier wants you to get information from Missy and Sacks, but please be careful. If what we suspect is true—that Franklin was mistaken for me—"

"Then the killer is still out there," I finish for him. "And might realize their mistake." The thought sends a chill through me that has nothing to do with the evening air. "Maybe I should stay here with you."

Jack shakes his head firmly. "Absolutely not. We need answers, and you and Maggie are our best chance at getting them." He takes my hands in his. "Besides, I have the entire Royal Guard on high alert, and these two fierce protectors." He gestures to Joe and Luma, who are now engaged in what appears to be a very gentle game of tug-of-war with Luma's favorite rope toy.

"Ferocious," Maggie deadpans.

"You know," Jack says, his expression softening as he looks at me, "I'm actually quite relieved not to be your date for this particular event." When I raise an eyebrow in question, he continues, "Movie premieres mean endless small talk with people who think being the Duke is just about wearing fancy clothes and cutting ribbons. I much prefer being your date for events that actually matter." His smile turns tender. "Like our wedding."

The mention of our wedding sends a flutter through my chest— part excitement, part panic, all complicated by the current murder investigation.

"If we ever agree on what kind of wedding we're having," I remind him, though I can't help returning his smile.

"We will," he says with a certainty I wish I shared. "After this case is solved, we'll sit down and find the perfect compromise. Something that honors tradition without making you feel like you're performing for strangers."

I'm about to respond when headlights sweep across the driveway, announcing Enrique's arrival. The town car rolls to a smooth stop in front of us, its black exterior gleaming in the fading light. Enrique emerges with his usual stoic expression, opening the rear door without a word.

"Right on time," Maggie says approvingly, checking her watch. "We should arrive just as the red carpet opens."

"Remember everything we reviewed about the film," she adds to me in a lower voice. "*Jules et Jim* is a French cinema classic about a love triangle, and Missy plays the modern Jeanne Moreau character in this remake."

"I know, I know," I assure her, though the truth is I've retained about ten percent of the film facts she drilled into me this afternoon. "French movie, complicated relationships, lots of artistic camera angles to comment on."

Jack chuckles, pulling me into a quick embrace. "You'll be brilliant," he whispers against my hair. "Just be yourself— well, yourself pretending to be someone with a magazine column."

"That's...not actually helpful advice," I inform him, but I return the hug fiercely, suddenly reluctant to leave him. "Stay safe. Don't let Joe eat anything from your plate, no matter how pathetic he looks."

"I would never fall for such transparent manipulation," Jack says with dignity, while we both know it's a complete lie.

Joe approaches for a proper goodbye, his massive head butting gently against my hip. I kneel down one last time, dress be damned, and wrap my arms around his neck. "Be good," I tell him softly. "Keep Jack and Luma safe for me."

He burps into my cheek, his breath still smelling like the

sugar cookies he ate, then gives me an apologetic look before stepping back to stand beside Jack.

"Ladies," Enrique says from beside the car, his voice as expressionless as his face. "We should depart if you wish to arrive on schedule."

"Of course," Maggie says, already sliding into the back seat with practiced grace.

I give Jack one last quick kiss. "I'll call if we learn anything important."

"And I'll call if Joe and Luma stage a coup and take over the castle," he promises.

With a final wave to the unlikely trio— a duke and two dogs silhouetted against the castle entrance— I climb into the car, my dress gathering around me like a pool of dark water. As Enrique pulls away, I watch through the rear window as Jack kneels between Joe and Luma, saying something to them that makes his face light up with laughter.

"Focus, Rebecca," Maggie says gently, touching my arm. "We have a murderer to catch."

"Right," I say, turning away from the window and toward whatever awaits us at the premiere. "Let's go see what we can find."

———

The premiere venue glows like a beacon against the night sky, its entrance swarming with photographers, journalists, and film industry people who all seem to know exactly what they're doing. I, on the other hand, am fighting the urge to check if I've somehow put my dress on backward as Enrique pulls the town car up to the red carpet. Through the tinted windows, I spot the trademark flash of cameras and the distinctive black-on-black outfits of the entertainment press corps we're supposed to be infiltrating tonight.

"We're here, ladies," Enrique announces, his voice as

expressionless as ever as he brings the vehicle to a perfect stop precisely where the red carpet begins. He turns slightly in his seat, his eyes meeting mine in the rearview mirror. "I will remain in the vicinity. Should you require extraction, simply call my direct line."

"Extraction?" I repeat, amused by his choice of words. "This is a film premiere, not a hostage situation."

The corner of Enrique's mouth twitches— the closest thing to a smile I've ever seen from him. "If the movies are to be believed, Ms. Orange, they can sometimes be one and the same."

Before I can respond to this unexpected bit of driver wisdom, Maggie nudges me toward the door that Enrique has opened. We step out into the cool evening air, the noise of the crowd hitting us like a physical wave.

"Rebecca! Maggie!"

I turn to see Zacharia waving frantically at us from behind a velvet rope that separates the general press from the more exclusive red-carpet area. His press credentials hang around his neck, looking slightly more worn than our pristine forgeries. He gestures urgently for us to join him.

"I saved you spots!" he calls as we approach. "Front row view of all the action!"

"Thanks, Zacharia," Maggie says, her voice the perfect blend of professional and friendly as we duck under the rope to join him. "Any sign of our... subjects of interest?"

"Missy arrived twenty minutes ago," he whispers, his eyes gleaming with excitement. "Made a grand entrance, of course. Sacks was right behind her, managing the press like a puppet master." He leans in closer, lowering his voice conspiratorially. "Do you really think she could be a murderer? I mean, she plays one in this movie, but in real life?" Before either of us can answer, he continues, "That would sell so many magazines!"

"We're just gathering information," I remind him. "And

don't forget—you're not allowed to say anything. This is all top secret."

"Mums the word!" Zacharia agrees. "The cocktail reception is already underway inside," he gestures toward the main doors. "That's your best chance to get dirt on Missy. Once the screening starts, they'll have her cordoned off in the VIP section."

We thank him and make our way inside, flashing our fake press badges with what I hope is convincing nonchalance. The security guard barely glances at them before waving us through, which is either a testament to Officer Basilier's connections or a concerning lapse in event security.

The reception area is a sea of elegant people in formal wear, their laughter blending with the soft classical music being played by a string quartet in the corner. Crystal chandeliers cast a warm glow over the scene, making everyone look airbrushed and perfect.

"I feel like I'm in a foreign country without a phrase book," I mutter to Maggie as we scan the room.

"Just smile and nod if anyone talks to you," she advises. "Most people at these events are just waiting for their turn to speak anyway."

My eyes lock on our targets almost immediately. Missy Adeline stands near the center of the room, a vision in a deep red gown that makes my black dress look like something you'd wear to take out the garbage. Sacks hovers at her elbow, his paisley bow tie somehow even more offensive than the shirt he wore at the castle. Paisley must be his trademark. Leave it to a publicist to pick the ugliest print as a branded fashion statement. Sacks and Missy are surrounded by a small group of admirers, all leaning in to catch Missy's every word.

"How do we get close without being recognized?" I whisper to Maggie. "They definitely saw our faces at the questioning."

Maggie purses her lips, thinking. "We could—"

"Wait," I interrupt, noticing something. "The catering staff. They're all wearing black." I gesture subtly toward the servers circulating with trays of champagne and hors d'oeuvres. Their simple black attire isn't identical to my dress, but in the dim lighting and general chaos, it's close enough.

"You're not seriously suggesting—"

"It's perfect," I insist. "I'll grab a tray, circle around behind them, and eavesdrop. You stay here and keep watch. If anyone gets suspicious, create a diversion."

"What kind of diversion?" Maggie asks, looking alarmed.

"I don't know. Spill something. Faint. Release a small animal. Use your imagination."

Before she can object further, I slip away toward the kitchen entrance, where I spot a server setting down an empty tray on a side table. With a quick glance around to ensure no one's watching, I casually pick it up and adopt what I hope is a server's professional stride.

Tray in hand, I weave through the crowd, nodding politely at guests while making my way toward Missy's group. I position myself just behind her, pretending to offer my empty tray to nearby guests who give me confused looks before moving on.

"...absolutely transformative experience," Missy is saying, her slight accent more pronounced than it was during questioning. "Playing Cathérine allowed me to explore the duality of feminine power and vulnerability in a way that felt almost..." she pauses dramatically, "transcendent."

"The early reviews are extremely positive," Sacks adds, his voice oozing with self-satisfaction. "Variety called it 'a tour de force performance that redefines a classic.'"

"It's just so difficult to focus on the film's release after such a traumatic experience," Missy continues, touching her throat delicately. "Being present at the Royal Masquerade when that poor Ambassador was murdered... I haven't slept properly since."

"Missy has been incredibly brave," Sacks interjects smoothly. "She's scheduled for multiple press interviews about the experience. The public is fascinated by her connection to the case."

"Naturally, I'm cooperating fully with the authorities," Missy adds. "Though reliving that night..." She shudders dramatically, and I have to resist the urge to roll my eyes.

Suddenly, Missy checks her diamond-encrusted watch and makes a small sound of dismay. "We should mingle with the other side of the room before the screening," she announces to her audience. "Do excuse us."

As Missy and Sacks glide away, I remain frozen in place, still holding my empty tray and pretending to be invisible. The group they've left behind collectively exhales, their postures relaxing instantly.

"God, that was exhausting," one-woman murmurs to her companion. "She's been going on like that all night."

"Did you see the early screening report?" a man in thick-framed glasses whispers. "It's a disaster. Critics are calling it 'a pretentious reimagining that misses the point of the original entirely.'"

"Her career's on life support after this," another adds. "That's probably why she's milking the murder connection so hard. She needs the publicity, any publicity."

"Sacks must be in panic mode," the first woman says. "You know how he operates—he'd do anything to keep her relevant."

I back away slowly, my mind racing with this new information. If Missy's career is in trouble and she and Sacks are desperate for publicity...

I turn too quickly and collide directly with someone, nearly dropping my tray. Looking up, I find myself staring into Missy Adeline's perfectly made-up face, her expression shifting from surprise to recognition in an instant.

"Ms. Orange?" Her perfectly sculpted eyebrows arch high.

"What are you doing here? Moonlighting as a caterer, or..." her eyes drop to my empty tray, then back to my face, "...a reporter?"

My mouth opens but no words come out. Before I can formulate a response, Maggie appears at my side as if materialized from thin air.

"There you are, Rebecca!" she exclaims with convincing relief. "I've been looking everywhere for you." She turns to Missy with a polished smile. "Ms. Adeline, how lovely to see you again. I'm afraid Rebecca was simply hungry and picked up a tray to gather some hors d'oeuvres. The service tonight is rather slow, isn't it?"

Missy's eyes narrow slightly, clearly not entirely convinced, but Sacks appears at her elbow before she can press further.

"Missy, darling, the director is asking for you," he says, then notices us and falters slightly. "Oh... hello."

"We were just leaving," Maggie says smoothly, taking the tray from my hands and setting it on a nearby table. "Enjoy the screening."

She steers me toward the exit with gentle but insistent pressure on my elbow. We maintain a dignified pace until we're through the doors, then practically sprint the remaining distance to the street.

"That was close," I gasp once we're safely outside.

"Too close," Maggie agrees. "But potentially worth it. Did you hear anything useful?"

"Actually, yes," I say, my breath forming small clouds in the cooling night air. "After Missy and Sacks walked away, I overheard the others talking. Apparently, the movie is terrible, and Missy's career is in serious trouble. They said she's 'milking the murder connection' for publicity."

Maggie's eyes widen. "You think they actually planned this? Killed the Ambassador just for the attention it would bring her?"

"It sounds crazy," I admit, "but people in desperate situations do desperate things, and Sacks strikes me as the type who'd do anything to protect his meal ticket."

We stand there in silence for a moment, the sounds of the premiere continuing behind us while we contemplate the possibility that a fading movie star and her ambitious publicist might have orchestrated a murder simply to generate headlines.

"We need to tell Officer Basilier," Maggie finally says. "This changes everything."

I nod, already reaching for my phone to call Enrique for our "extraction." "And here I thought Hollywood was just about pretending to kill people, not actually doing it."

CHAPTER
Nine

THE MORNING SUN catches on my engagement ring as I spread a thick flannel blanket across the dewy grass. The jewels send prisms of light dancing across Joe's fur, and he looks up at me with his big, earnest eyes. He's been aloof all morning, and I think he's still mad about missing out on the chance to go to the premiere last night. But he licks my hand with a begrudging kiss that says he can't stay mad at me. Next to me, Jack arranges our own morning spread— fresh pastries from *Le Petit Scone*, thermoses of pumpkin-spiced coffee, and sliced squash that's already attracting the curious gaze of a nearby alpaca. Luma trots at his heel. Behind us, Alfredo, the giraffe, stretches his long neck toward the sky, impatient for his breakfast.

"Patience, Alfredo," Jack calls out, his voice carrying across the sanctuary grounds. "Your pasta will be ready momentarily."

I can't help but smile at the absurdity of our situation— a Duke preparing breakfast for a giraffe who refuses to eat anything but pasta.

"Here," Jack says, handing me a steaming mug of coffee.

"You look like you need this after your undercover adventure last night."

I accept the mug gratefully, wrapping both hands around its warmth. "Is it that obvious? I feel like I haven't slept at all."

"You were tossing and turning all night," he confirms, settling beside me on the blanket. "Joe gave up and moved to the foot of the bed around three in the morning."

Joe, hearing his name, abandons his inspection of the picnic basket to flop down between us with a dramatic sigh. His massive body takes up more than his fair share of the blanket, but neither of us minds. Luma prances around the perimeter of our setup, her collie instincts compelling her to circle the "herd" before she'll allow herself to relax.

"Come here, girl," Jack pats the blanket, and Luma immediately responds, trotting over to nestle against his side.

For a moment, we sit in comfortable silence, sipping our coffee while the castle's exotic residents go about their morning routines around us. Alfredo has finally received his bowl of pasta— cooked al dente and mixed with raw eggs for protein— and is delicately picking at it with his long blue tongue. The alpacas graze nearby, occasionally lifting their heads to observe us with mild curiosity.

I twist my engagement ring around my finger, a nervous habit I've developed since Jack proposed. The antique diamond catches the light again, sending another spray of tiny rainbows across the blanket. It still feels surreal sometimes— me, Rebecca Orange, former zookeeper from San Diego, engaged to a duke, solving murders, and having picnic breakfasts at a castle.

"Tell me about the premiere," Jack says, breaking into my thoughts as he unpacks a box of croissants. "Was Missy Adeline as dramatic in person as she is on screen?"

"More," I say with a laugh, accepting a croissant and tearing off a piece. "She was working that red carpet like she was born on it. All smiles and poses and perfect sound bites for the press." I toss the piece of croissant to Joe, who catches it mid-air with surprising delicacy for such a large animal. "It was exhausting just watching her."

"And the undercover operation? Any useful intelligence gathered before you were discovered?" Jack's tone is light, but I can see the concern in his eyes. He'd been worried about me attending the premiere, given our suspicion that the Ambassador's killer might have been targeting him instead.

"Well, before Missy caught me pretending to be a server—"

"You did what?" Jack nearly chokes on his coffee.

"It seemed like a good idea at the time," I defend myself. "Anyway, I overheard some interesting gossip. Apparently, Missy's new film is terrible, and her career is tanking. She and Sacks are supposedly 'milking' the murder connection for publicity."

Jack frowns, breaking off a piece of his own croissant for Luma. "That's a rather disturbing motive for murder, isn't it? Kill someone just to get press coverage?"

"People have done worse for fame," I point out, watching as Alfredo stretches his neck toward a low-hanging branch. "But Officer Basilier is looking into it. We called her during the car ride home and gave her a full report."

"Hmm," Jack murmurs, his expression thoughtful. "It does seem far-fetched, but we can't rule anything out yet."

I take another sip of coffee, wondering if we'll ever know the truth about Ambassador Franklin's death. The investigation has dominated our lives for the past few days, pushing aside other important conversations— like the one we've been avoiding about our wedding.

"I can't imagine it," I say after a moment, watching Missy's face take shape in my memory. "Being the center of attention like that, having cameras flash in your face, everyone watching your every move, analyzing your outfit, your hair, your expressions..."

"You might want to get used to it," Jack says gently, his hand finding mine on the blanket. "You're marrying into the Royal family. A certain amount of public attention comes with the territory."

I twist my ring again, the weight of it suddenly heavier. "I know. It's just... different when I think about it in terms of our wedding. It feels more personal, more invasive somehow."

Jack's thumb traces small circles on the back of my hand. "Speaking of our wedding," he begins, and I feel my stomach tighten slightly. "I was hoping we might finally settle on what kind of celebration we're going to have. The planner keeps calling Maggie for decisions, and we've yet to give her any concrete direction."

"I know, I know," I sigh, leaning back on one elbow and gazing up at the clear morning sky. "It's just such a big decision. And every option seems to come with a thousand complicated considerations."

Joe shifts position, resting his massive head on my lap as if sensing my discomfort with the topic. I scratch behind his ears automatically, drawing comfort from his warm presence.

"What are you afraid of, really?" Jack asks, his voice soft with understanding rather than accusation.

I look at him, at this man who has somehow become the center of my world in less than a year, and feel a wave of conflicting emotions crash over me. "I'm afraid I can't give you the wedding you deserve," I admit finally. "I don't want to embarrass you in front of your family and your people. If we do something big and public, it's guaranteed I'll trip over my dress or say the wrong thing or look like an imposter in a world I wasn't born into."

Jack sets down his coffee and turns to face me fully. "Rebecca, all I want is to marry you. The rest is just... details."

"But they're not just details to the Queen, are they? Or to the people of Monrovia? You've said it yourself— a royal wedding is a statement, a tradition, a public event." I run my fingers through Joe's thick fur, anchoring myself. "I love you completely, Jack. I want to marry you more than I've ever wanted anything. I just... I worry about everything that comes with it. And clearly you feel like you owe the people transparency, and a big event. I don't want to stand in the way of that."

Jack is quiet for a moment, watching Alfredo finish his pasta while the alpacas edge closer to our blanket, curious about our breakfast spread. Finally, he looks back at me, his eyes reflecting the morning sunlight.

"If I weren't a Duke and didn't owe the public anything... and you could have any wedding in the world," he asks, "what would it be?"

I breathe out slowly, feeling a weight lift at the simple question. "Honestly, this— right here. A picnic with a giraffe, just us." I gesture to the sanctuary around us, to Joe and Luma, to the simple beauty of the morning. "Something small and intimate where we could actually be present with each other, not performing for hundreds of guests we barely know."

Jack's expression softens, but I can see the conflict in his eyes. "The Queen would hate it," he says with a rueful smile. "They've been looking forward to a grand royal wedding since I was born, I think. They only have one child of their own—my cousin— and she's too young. She won't be getting married for quite some time."

"I know," I acknowledge.

"And running off to elope would probably stir even more press uproar than a traditional ceremony," he continues, voicing what we both know is true. "The tabloids would have a field day speculating about why we chose to marry in secret."

"Would that be so terrible?" I ask, genuinely curious. "To choose something that makes us happy instead of what's expected?"

Jack tears a piece of croissant into smaller bits, tossing them onto the blanket for Luma to find. "It's not just about tradition," he says after a moment. "It's about what I owe the people as their Duke. The royal family exists to serve Monrovia, to maintain continuity and stability. Royal weddings give people joy, something to celebrate together. They connect the monarchy to the people in a tangible way. I was a poor leader for so long— I feel I failed them and took my position for granted, long before you met me..."

I watch his face as he speaks, seeing the weight of responsibility he carries— a weight I'm still learning to understand. "Jack," I say, placing my hand on his, "don't you think you've given enough? You opened the castle to visitors, invested in the village, and established the animal sanctuary. You stopped being a wild bachelor on yachts and fancy vacations to pour yourself into this role." I lean closer, lowering my voice even though there's no one around to hear us but the animals. "Maybe it's time to do what you want?"

His eyes meet mine, and I see a vulnerability there that he rarely shows to anyone else. "What makes you think I don't want a traditional royal wedding?"

"The way you tense up whenever Maggie shows us another three-thousand-person guest list. The relief on your face when I suggested something smaller."

Joe shifts his position, rolling onto his back in a silent request for belly rubs. Jack obliges, reaching over to scratch the massive dog's stomach. "Am I that easy to read?"

"Only to me," I assure him. "And possibly to Joe."

As if to confirm, Joe lets out a contented groan under Jack's ministrations.

"If you could get married in the way that makes *you* happy and didn't owe the people anything," I ask, turning his earlier question back on him, "what would it be?"

Jack stares off toward the grazing alpacas, and I watch him struggle to bridge the gap between duty and desire. The morning light catches the silver in his hair, reminding me of how the Ambassador's similar coloring had initially made my heart stop when I found his body. The thought that someone might have been targeting Jack instead still chills me.

"I don't know," he says finally, the simple admission clearly costing him. "I've spent so long thinking about what I should do, what's expected of me, what serves the monarchy best... I'm not sure I know what I want anymore."

There's such honest confusion in his voice that I feel my throat tighten with emotion. I scoot closer to him on the blanket, displacing Joe, who gives me a reproachful look before settling against my other side.

"Then maybe that's what we need to figure out," I suggest. "Not what the Queen wants, not what tradition demands, not even what I want. But what would make you, Jack—not the Duke of Atwood, just Jack—happy on his wedding day."

"Aren't weddings about the bride?"

"I want ours to be about both of us," I say.

Jack looks at me with such tenderness that I almost can't bear it. "What would make me happiest is seeing you comfortable and happy. If a huge royal spectacle would make you miserable, then it wouldn't bring me joy either."

"But that's not an answer," I press gently. "That's just deflecting and making it about me instead of the people. What about *you*?"

Luma, perhaps sensing the emotional tension, moves to lie across Jack's lap, looking up at him with adoring eyes. He strokes her fur thoughtfully.

"I suppose..." he begins slowly, "I'd want something that honors the significance of the occasion without turning it into a performance. Something that includes the people who truly matter to us, that respects tradition without being enslaved to it." He looks around at the sanctuary, at Alfredo now watching us curiously, at the castle visible on the hill in the distance. "Something that represents who we are together, not just our titles or positions."

"That sounds perfect," I say, leaning my head against his shoulder.

"But it doesn't solve our practical dilemma," he points out. "The expectations still exist."

"Maybe there's a middle ground," I suggest. "Something that isn't three thousand strangers in a cathedral but also isn't just us and the animals."

Jack wraps his arm around me, pulling me closer. "We'll figure it out," he promises. "We have time."

As if to punctuate his statement, Alfredo chooses that moment to approach our blanket, his long legs carrying him with surprising grace across the grass. He extends his neck toward the fruit platter, eyeing the apple slices with interest despite his usual pasta preference.

"No, you don't," Jack laughs, gently shooing the giraffe away. "You've had your breakfast already."

Alfredo seems unbothered by the rejection, turning his attention to a nearby tree instead. Joe watches the giraffe with mild interest before closing his eyes, content in the morning sun.

We sit in comfortable silence for a moment, the weight of our unresolved wedding plans still hovering between us, but somehow less daunting than before. There's something about being here, surrounded by the sanctuary's peaceful residents, that puts our human concerns in perspective.

"Whatever we decide," I say finally, "we'll decide together. And it will be perfect because it will be ours."

Jack presses a kiss to the top of my head. "How did I get so lucky?" he murmurs against my hair.

"You hired a zookeeper with a massive dog and question-able fashion sense," I remind him. "Clearly, you have impec-cable taste."

His laughter rings out across the sanctuary, startling a

nearby peacock into an indignant squawk. And for this moment at least, the murder investigation, the wedding dilemma, and all our other worries feel distant and manageable. We have each other, we have our animals, and we have this perfect morning.

Everything else can wait.

CHAPTER

Ten

THE CASTLE PARLOR feels like a pressure cooker this morning, all polished wood and tension thick enough to slice. Maggie sits ramrod straight beside me on the antique settee, her tablet balanced on her knee, while Joe stretches out at my feet with a deceptive casualness that doesn't fool me— he can sense the strain in the room as clearly as I can. Across from us, Prime Minister Floridán and his wife Geneviève occupy matching armchairs, a united front separated by an ornate side table. The Prime Minister keeps checking his watch, his impressive mustache twitching with impatience, while Geneviève's hands remain perfectly folded in her lap, only the whiteness of her knuckles betraying her nerves.

"We appreciate you making time for us today," Maggie begins, her voice carrying that perfect blend of authority and warmth she's mastered over years of castle diplomacy. "We understand your schedules are quite demanding."

"Yes, well, when one receives a formal request through the Duke's office, one can hardly refuse," Prime Minister Floridán replies, emphasizing the word "Duke" with barely concealed disdain. "Though I must say, we've already spoken with the police. I'm not sure what a second interview with castle staff might accomplish."

"Royal Investigators," I correct automatically, earning a sidelong glance from Maggie that says please behave. "And we're close to resolving the case. We just need to clarify a few things with you both, if you don't mind."

"Of course we don't mind," Geneviève says, subtly elbowing her husband in the ribs. "Anything for the Duke and his Royal Investigators, one of whom will soon be a duchess."

Joe shifts at my feet, his massive head coming to rest against my ankle in what I recognize as his subtle signal: someone in this room is nervous. I follow his gaze to Ginevième, whose composed expression doesn't quite reach her eyes.

"Perhaps we could start with your movements on the night of the masquerade," Maggie suggests, tapping her tablet to pull up notes. "Where were you when the lights went out?"

"I was by the dessert table," the Prime Minister answers without hesitation. "Sampling those little chocolate things with the gold flakes. Absurdly expensive, I imagine, but that's royalty for you— all flash, no substance."

I bite my tongue, reminding myself that insulting Jack's dessert choices isn't a crime.

"And you, Mrs. Floridán?" I ask, directing my attention to Geneviève.

She blinks twice before answering, a tell I've noticed in people who are carefully choosing their words. "I was on the terrace. Getting some air."

"Alone?" Maggie probes gently.

Geneviève's gaze flickers to her husband before returning to us. "Yes."

There's something in the way her upper lip twitches that makes me think she isn't being truthful. *Liar!*, I think, but keep my expression neutral. Joe's ears perk up slightly, another tell from my canine detective that something's off.

"Did either of you interact with Ambassador Franklin that evening?" I ask, watching both of their faces carefully.

The Prime Minister scoffs. "Why would I? The man was Antanaro's puppet, pushing for this ridiculous compromise on Île des Lilas."

"And you, Mrs. Floridán?" I persist, noticing how she's suddenly become very interested in adjusting the sleeve of her blouse.

"I... may have exchanged pleasantries," she admits. "Nothing of substance."

The Prime Minister's head swivels toward his wife, surprise evident in his expression. "You didn't mention—"

"It wasn't worth mentioning, dear," she says smoothly. "Merely a diplomatic greeting."

I glance at Maggie, who gives me the slightest nod. We're both thinking the same thing: there's more here than pleasantries.

"Mrs. Floridán," I begin, leaning forward slightly, "we've heard from several sources that you and Ambassador Franklin knew each other before your marriage. Is that true?"

The temperature in the room seems to drop ten degrees. The Prime Minister's mustache practically bristles with sudden tension, while Geneviève's composure cracks just enough to reveal a flash of alarm before she recovers.

"That was a very long time ago," she says carefully. "We were students together at university. A brief... acquaintance."

"I won't have you questioning my wife about something so improper—"

Geneviève's perfectly manicured nails dig into the fabric of the armchair. "It's fine, darling. I had my life before I met you. They're allowed to ask about it."

"You dated the Ambassador," I say, not as a question but a statement. "Didn't you?"

The silence that follows is so complete I can hear Joe's breathing at my feet. Geneviève's shoulders slump slightly, the first real crack in her poised facade.

"Yes," she finally admits. "For about a year during our final year of university. It was nothing serious, and it ended amicably when he took a position abroad."

The Prime Minister's face has turned an alarming shade of red. "How dare you bring up ancient history! This is an attack!" His voice rises with each word.

"I promise you," Ginevière says to us, ignoring her husband's growing anger. "This isn't relevant to your investigation. It was more than twenty years ago."

"It becomes relevant," Maggie interjects smoothly, "when you fail to disclose a personal connection to the victim during a murder investigation.

"I didn't kill him!" Geneviève's composure finally shatters, the first signs of stress appearing on her brow. "Why would I? Because of a college romance that ended decades ago?"

"Or perhaps because he was pushing for a compromise your husband violently opposes?" I suggest, turning to the Prime Minister, whose complexion now resembles an overripe tomato. "You're against the 50/50 split on Île des Lilas, aren't you, Prime Minister?"

"Of course I am!" he thunders, pounding a fist on the arm of his chair with enough force to make Joe lift his head in alert. "That island belongs to Monrovia! It's been part of our territory for centuries! This 'compromise' is nothing but a surrender to international pressure."

"So Ambassador Franklin's death benefits your political position," Maggie notes, her voice remaining calm despite the Prime Minister's outburst.

"That's absurd," he sputters. "I oppose the compromise on principle, but I wouldn't—" He stops abruptly, as if realizing how his words might sound.

"Darling," Geneviève says quietly. "Remember what we talked about."

The Prime Minister takes a deep breath, then settles back into his chair. "I am an elected official," he says the word 'elected' like it's part of a personal mantra. "The people chose me to represent them. Unlike your precious Duke, I have been chosen to express their will— not appointed due to who my parents were. I have every right to look out for the well-being of my country. This investigation feels, to me, as if you are searching for a smoking gun to discredit me by going through my wife's history. You won't find one."

"That's not what's happening here, Mister Prime Minister," Maggie says, raising her hands in the air. "We only ask questions in the hopes of eliminating you both as suspects. And we deeply appreciate your cooperation."

"Now that we know you were both occupied at the time of the murder, we can look at other people," I say, lying through my teeth. I won't say it out loud, but I find the Prime Minister's anger to be highly suspicious. Maybe he killed Ambassador Franklin out of jealousy over an old affair. "Speaking of other suspects," I ask, changing tack, "What about Missy Adeline? Did either of you see her location around the ballroom in the moments before the Ambassador was killed?"

The Prime Minister's nostrils flare. "That woman is a menace. Always showing up at political events, using her celebrity status to push Antanaro's agenda. She has no business involving herself in diplomatic matters she doesn't understand."

"She's an activist," Ginevière interjects, her voice regaining some of its steadiness. "She's entitled to her opinions."

"Her opinions," the Prime Minister retorts, "are dangerous propaganda wrapped in a pretty package. And her presence at a Monrovian royal event was offensive under the circumstances."

"The circumstances being the island vote?" I clarify.

"Obviously," he snaps. "She's been giving interviews for months about how Antanaro deserves full control of the island. As if an actress should have any say in territorial disputes!"

I notice Geneviève watching her husband with an expression I can't quite read— concern, perhaps, or calculation. Whatever it is, the dynamic between them has shifted since the revelation of her past with Franklin.

"I think we have enough for now," Maggie says, rising gracefully from the settee. "Thank you both for your time."

The Prime Minister stands abruptly. "This interview is over. And I would appreciate it being kept confidential. The last thing we need is tabloid speculation about ancient history." He shoots a pointed look at his wife before striding toward the door.

Geneviève follows more slowly, pausing beside me. "It really was nothing," she says quietly. "The past is the past."

But as I watch them leave— the Prime Minister storming ahead, Geneviève following with her shoulders now slightly curved inward— I can't help thinking that sometimes the past isn't as dead as we'd like it to be. Sometimes it's waiting for us, like a knife in the dark.

———

"Well, that was illuminating," I say once we're safely out of the parlor, Joe padding quietly beside me as we make our way down the castle's main corridor. The morning sunlight streams through the tall windows, casting long rectangles of light across the polished floor. "Nothing says 'we have a healthy marriage' quite like discovering your wife dated the murder victim two decades ago."

Maggie taps furiously on her tablet, her fingers flying

across the screen. "I'm adding Geneviève to our primary suspect list. The undisclosed relationship with Ambassador Franklin is significant."

"And did you see the Prime Minister's face?" I lower my voice, though we're well out of earshot now. "I thought his mustache was going to catch fire from the heat of his anger. Maybe he wanted the Ambassador dead because he was jealous over a recently-discovered past affair?"

"Political motivation, personal jealousy—take your pick," Maggie agrees. "Either way, they both had reasons to want Franklin gone."

Joe stops suddenly, his massive head swiveling toward a side corridor where the faint sound of cleaning supplies clanking against each other announces someone's approach. A moment later, Monique appears, pushing her cleaning cart with its neatly arranged bottles and cloths. Her crisp uniform looks as perfectly pressed as ever, not a wrinkle in sight despite the morning's work.

"Miss Orange, Miss Lefevere," she greets us with a small nod, her French accent more pronounced than usual. "And Joe, of course." She gives my dog a respectful distance— Monique has never quite adjusted to Joe's size, though she's warmed to his presence in the castle.

"Monique," I return warmly. "How are you this morning?"

"Very well, thank you." Her eyes dart between us, a knowing look crossing her features. "You have been speaking with the Prime Minister and his wife, yes?"

Maggie and I exchange glances. "News travels fast in the castle," I observe.

Monique's perfectly shaped eyebrows lift slightly. "The castle has many ears, Miss Orange. And many eyes." She adjusts her cleaning gloves, seeming to deliberate before continuing. "Perhaps I should not say this, but... it is about the night of the murder."

I feel my pulse quicken. "What about it?"

Monique glances down the corridor in both directions before stepping closer, her voice dropping to just above a whisper. "I was cleaning the terrace doors that evening. The glass needed extra attention because of fingerprints from guests going in and out." She pauses, her expression serious. "I saw Mrs. Floridán and Ambassador Franklin there during the masquerade. They were... having a conversation."

"What kind of conversation?" Maggie asks, her tablet now forgotten at her side.

"It was..." Monique searches for the word, her brow furrowed. "Intense. Not angry, but very serious. They stood close together, speaking quietly." She demonstrates with her hands, showing how their heads were bent toward each other. "Like people who know each other well, you understand?"

Joe has moved to sit directly in front of Monique, his eyes fixed on her face with that unnervingly intelligent gaze that makes some people nervous. Monique, to her credit, merely acknowledges him with a slight nod before continuing.

"The Ambassador, he touched her arm at one point," she adds. "Just briefly. She pulled away as if it burned her."

"Did you hear what they were saying?" I press gently.

Monique shakes her head. "Only fragments. Something about 'the past' and 'what might have been.' Then Mrs. Floridán said something that sounded like 'we cannot change it now.'" She shrugs apologetically. "My English is good, but they were speaking very quietly."

"How long did this conversation last?" Maggie's professional tone has returned, though I can see the excitement in her eyes.

"Perhaps five minutes? Then Mrs. Floridán went inside. The Ambassador stayed on the terrace for a moment, looking..." she gestures vaguely, "troubled. Then he also went back to the ballroom." Monique glances at her watch. "This was perhaps twenty minutes before the lights went out and the... incident."

"And Geneviève claimed she was alone on the terrace," I murmur, more to myself than to the others. "She lied to us."

"And to her husband, it seems," Maggie adds. "He appeared genuinely surprised when she mentioned even speaking to the Ambassador."

Joe makes a soft huffing sound that I've come to interpret as his version of "I told you so." He knew something was off during the interview— his canine instincts for deception rarely fail.

"Thank you, Monique," I say sincerely. "This is extremely helpful."

She nods, her expression serious. "I hope it helps find who did this terrible thing. The castle should be a place of celebration for your wedding, not..." she trails off, shaking her head.

"We'll find who did it," I promise, with more confidence than I actually feel.

As Monique continues down the corridor with her cart, Maggie turns to me, her eyes bright with that particular gleam she gets when puzzle pieces are falling into place.

"You okay?" I ask, laughing at the way she's frozen in place.

"I have an idea," she says, already pulling out her phone. "I need to call Zacharia."

"Why would you—"

"I'll explain later," Maggie says, putting her phone up to her ear. "Meet me at *Café de Flore* in two hours!" With that, she runs down the hall, disappearing around the corner.

Joe nudges my hand with his cold nose, reminding me of his presence. I scratch behind his ears, feeling the usual rush of affection for this enormous furry detective. "What do you think, buddy? Should we feed the alpacas then head to the village?"

Joe tilts his head, his expression somehow managing to

convey both deep wisdom and complete confusion, which pretty much sums up how I feel about this case too.

"Come on," I tell him, turning toward the castle grounds.

As we head outside into the crisp, autumn day, the wind picks up over the castle grounds. I hope Maggie's onto something, I think, praying that she's solved the case.

CHAPTER
Eleven

CAFÉ DE FLORE looks like it's been possessed by the Halloween spirit, and I mean that in the best possible way. Orange and black garlands drape from every available surface, paper stars drip from the ceiling, and tiny carved pumpkins line the windowsills, their flickering electric candles casting spooky shadows across the walls. Joe hesitates at the entrance, his massive frame blocking the doorway as he takes in the transformation of our usually quaint local café into what can only be described as a festive haunted house. "It's still the same place, buddy," I assure him, gently tugging his leash. "Just with more... ambiance."

Joe gives me a skeptical look but follows me inside, his paws clicking against the wooden floor as we navigate through the familiar place, which has been transformed for the impending arrival of All Souls Day. The café is surprisingly empty for this time of day, with only one couple tucked in the corner sharing what appears to be a cauldron-shaped mug of hot chocolate between them.

Jocelyn glides over to us, her usual quiet demeanor somehow enhanced by the witch's hat perched atop her head.

The pointy black accessory should look ridiculous, but she somehow makes it seem elegant.

"Rebecca, Joe," she greets us softly. "Your usual table is ready. The others haven't arrived yet."

"Thanks, Jocelyn," I say, following her to our favorite corner spot near the window. "The place looks amazing. You've really outdone yourself this year."

She offers a small, pleased smile. "All Souls Day is my favorite holiday. It deserves proper celebration. I've even stolen some of your American Halloween decorating ideas." She winks at me, and then her eyes drift around the café with unmistakable pride. "I've just baked some new seasonal treats. Would you like to try them while you wait?"

"Are they dog-friendly?" I ask, glancing down at Joe, who has already settled himself beneath the table, his massive head poking out like a furry submarine surfacing from the depths.

"Of course," Jocelyn says. "I made pumpkin-shaped biscuits with carob chips for Joe. And for you, perhaps our new All Souls Day latte? It's cinnamon-pumpkin with ghost-shaped marshmallows."

"Sold," I tell her. "And we'll be five total when everyone arrives."

She nods and drifts away, her movements almost ethereal in the dimly lit café . I settle into my chair, absently scratching behind Joe's ears as I check my phone. No updates from Maggie yet. I've also invited Jack to join us, just in case Maggie's cracked the case.

The bell above the door chimes, and I look up to see Jack enter with Luma trotting at his heels. His eyes find mine immediately, a smile spreading across his face that still makes my heart do ridiculous things in my chest. Luma spots Joe and makes a beeline for him, wiggling under the table to greet her massive friend with enthusiastic nuzzles.

"Sorry I'm late," Jack says, bending to kiss my cheek before taking the seat beside me. "Royal duties. Apparently, there's a crisis about the napkin colors for next month's charity dinner."

"Sounds traumatic," I say, patting his hand sympathetically. "How ever did you manage?"

"I delegated," he admits with a grin. "Told them to pick whatever colors don't clash with the centerpieces and left before anyone could ask me what a centerpiece is."

"The perfect royal response," I laugh. "Very diplomatic."

Jack glances around the café , taking in the decorations. "Wow. Jocelyn's really embracing the season, isn't she?"

"It's her favorite holiday. I think she's been planning this since last November."

Jocelyn returns with my latte— a steaming mug topped with whipped cream and marshmallows shaped like tiny ghosts— and a plate of dog treats for Joe. The biscuits are indeed shaped like pumpkins, with carob chip eyes and mouths that make them look eerily expressive.

"Thank you," I say, accepting the mug gratefully. "This looks amazing."

"The Duke might enjoy our special apple cider," Jocelyn suggests. "It's served warm with cinnamon sticks and star anise."

"That sounds perfect," Jack agrees.

The bell chimes again, and Maggie bustles in, her arms full of folders and her tablet tucked precariously under her chin. She looks like she's about to drop everything, so Jack jumps up to help her, relieving her of several thick manila envelopes.

"Thank you," she breathes, collapsing into the chair across from us. "I swear these get heavier every time I carry them."

"What exactly are 'these'?" I ask, eyeing the stack of folders now spread across our table.

"Information," Maggie says simply, her eyes gleaming with that particular excitement she gets when she's onto something. "Zacharia came through in a big way." She smiles at Jack. "Oh good, you're joining us!"

"I was invited in case you solved the case," Jack says, petting Luma's ears.

Maggie winces. "Don't get your hopes up, I'm afraid. I think I've only thrown another wrinkle in the timeline."

Jocelyn approaches again, this time with Jack's cider and a questioning look for Maggie. "The usual lavender tea?"

"Yes, please," Maggie says. "And whatever seasonal pastry you'd recommend. I haven't eaten since breakfast."

"The ghost meringues are particularly good today," Jocelyn suggests. "And the pumpkin tarts with maple glaze."

"One of each," Maggie decides. "Actually, bring a selection for the table. We might be here a while."

Once Jocelyn departs, Maggie leans forward, her voice dropping despite the nearly empty cafe. "You won't believe what Zacharia found."

"Wait until we get our treats," I say, taking a sip of my latte. The cinnamon-pumpkin flavor is perfect— spicy and sweet without being cloying. "This is too good to rush."

Maggie sighs but sits back, drumming her fingers impatiently on the table. Jack sips his cider, making an appreciative sound. One thing I've learned about Maggie is that she hates waiting— she's always been a woman who buzzes around without any patience for delays.

"This is excellent," he says. "I should have the kitchen staff come learn from Jocelyn."

"She'd never share her recipes," I tell him. "I've been trying to get her pumpkin bread formula for months."

"You two are killing me right now," Maggie says, rolling her eyes. "How can you think about treats at a time like this?"

Under the table, Joe and Luma have settled into a comfortable pile, with Luma curled up against Joe's massive side. The sound of Joe's tail thumping against the floor tells me he's enjoying his pumpkin treats.

Jocelyn returns with a three-tiered tray filled with Halloween-themed pastries: ghost-shaped meringues dusted with powdered sugar, miniature pumpkin tarts topped with maple glaze, chocolate cupcakes decorated to look like cauldrons complete with green "potion" frosting, and bat-shaped cookies with licorice details.

"This is incredible," I say, marveling at the display. "Did you make all of these yourself?"

Jocelyn nods, a hint of pride breaking through her usual reserved demeanor. "All Souls Day has always been special to me. It's when the veil between worlds is thinnest." She arranges Maggie's tea beside the tray. "When anything is possible."

"It's more than just costumes and candy, isn't it?" Jack asks with a grin. "I've been trying to explain to Rebecca why All Souls Day is different from her American Halloween, but I haven't convinced her yet."

Beside him, Maggie taps her foot on the floor, eager to get this chit-chat over with so she can share what she learned from Zacharia.

"It's similar to Halloween, but with an added twist," Jocelyn confirms. "It's about remembering those who came before us, honoring their memory, and recognizing that their spirits are still with us in some way." Her eyes drift to the elaborate altar she's set up in the corner of the café , decorated with marigolds, candles, and framed photographs of what I assume are her loved ones who have passed.

"It's about fate and destiny too," Maggie adds, finally joining the conversation. Maggie can never resist sharing facts about Monrovian heritage with me. Her eyes follow Jocelyn's gaze to the altar. "Believing in magic again, even just for one night. That's what makes All Souls Day special."

Jocelyn looks at Maggie with surprise and appreciation. "Exactly. Not many people understand that." She smiles—a real, full smile this time—before gliding away to attend to the couple in the corner.

"It's beautiful," Jack says, his expression thoughtful as he regards the altar. "Remembering those who came before us. Honoring their legacy."

I know he's thinking of his own family legacy, the weight of royal tradition he carries. I reach for his hand under the table, giving it a gentle squeeze.

"Speaking of honoring the dead," Maggie adds impatiently. "The Ambassador might quite like to have his murder avenged before the holiday arrives."

"I'll take that as my cue," Jocelyn says, laughing kindly and heading back toward the register.

"So," I say, turning back to Maggie. "What did you learn from Zacharia?"

Maggie glances around once more, then opens the top folder and spreads its contents across the table. Magazine clippings, newspaper articles, and what seems like surveillance photographs spill out, all featuring one familiar face: Missy Adeline.

"It was something the Prime Minister said that bothered me…" she answers, pointing at the photographs. "He said Missy is present at every political event she can get into, which seems odd for a movie star."

"It's true," Jack confirms. "I've seen her many times myself." He glances at my concerned expression. It's not lost on me that Missy Adeline is gorgeous. "But I hardly take notice," he adds coyly. "She's so ugly it's hard to look at her for long."

I slap his arm as Maggie continues. "Our magazines don't cover her as much as the tabloids in her home country. But Zacharia has contacts at entertainment magazines in Antanaro who owed him favors, so he asked for anything they had on her that wasn't publicly known. They were able to email them over and he printed them out for me, plus a few clippings he had saved in his archives."

I pick up one of the clippings— a grainy photo of what appears to be a diplomatic reception in some ornate government building. It takes me a moment to spot Missy, partially obscured by a large potted plant, dressed in a server's uniform much like the one I'd impersonated at the premiere.

"What am I looking at?" I ask, holding up the photo.

"That," Maggie says triumphantly, "is Missy Adeline at a closed-door meeting between Antanaran and Russian diplomats three years ago. She wasn't invited as a celebrity. She's just… there."

Jack leans closer, examining the photo with newfound interest. "Are you sure that's her?"

"Positive," Maggie confirms. "And it's not just this one event." She spreads more photos across the table. "Here she is as a backup dancer at a political fundraiser. Here as a photographer's assistant at a summit meeting. Here as part of the cleaning crew at the Monrovian embassy in Antanaro. These ones are from years ago before she was famous. This was back when she was a nobody. Before she hit it big. I think—Rebecca, I think she was hired to go to these events when she was a starving actor."

"Who would hire her for that?" I think out loud.

"It gets weirder," Maggie leans in, whispering. "Once she got famous, she became an activist. She was at every event she could attend." She pushes another pile of photos toward me.

I sort through the images, a pattern emerging that sends a chill down my spine despite the warm café atmosphere. "These are all political events. Diplomatic functions. Government meetings."

"Exactly," Maggie says, her voice buzzing with excitement. "And there are hundreds more examples. Zacharia's contacts have been tracking this for years, compiling evidence but never publishing because they couldn't confirm why she was there. They have a theory, but Zacharia said they won't publish the story until they're sure because the damages could be huge. Rebecca, his contacts think she's--"

I pause, the words feeling ridiculous even as I say them. "A *spy*?"

The word hangs in the air between us, heavy with implication.

I turn to Jack, dumbfounded. "Is that possible?"

Jack sets down his cider, his expression serious. "Anything's possible," he says slowly. "Spies aren't all James Bond. We've received reports of staff being bribed to provide information... It *would* explain a lot. Her extreme nationalism. Her conveniently timed presence at the masquerade, right before an important vote on the island dispute... In fact, I seem to recall she pushed quite hard for the invite, didn't she, Maggie?"

"Not her," Maggie shakes her head. "*Sacks.* He wouldn't leave me alone about it. He must have called twenty times to get her on the list."

"It still doesn't explain why she'd kill Ambassador Franklin instead of, say, the Prime Minister, who opposes Antanaro's interests."

"That's true," Jack agrees. "The Ambassador was a member of Antanaro. There's no way they'd send one of their spies to kill their own man. What a strange move that would be!"

"What about Sacks?" I ask, turning the question over in my mind. "He was the one who pushed for the invitation. Maybe he wanted to kill the Ambassador. But why?"

We fall silent, each lost in our own thoughts as we absently pick at the Halloween treats. The ghost meringue dissolves on my tongue, sweet and insubstantial— just like our theories.

"We need to find out more about Missy's movements on

the night of the murder," Jack says finally. "Where exactly she was when the lights went out."

Maggie nods, already making notes on her tablet. "I'll contact Officer Basilier about interviewing Missy again."

"I'll do some digging as well," Jack says, nodding in agreement. "If Missy's been a spy for Antanaro, someone in my cabinet might have gotten wind of her movements as well. But it still doesn't make sense she'd want to kill the Ambassador. They were on the same team, after all."

I take another sip of my latte, the ghost marshmallows now melted into the whipped cream. "You won't like my other most likely suspect," I tell him, shaking my head.

"What?" Jack says, suddenly worried.

"The Prime Minister," I say, telling him what Maggie and I suspect. "His wife used to date the Ambassador. And according to a witness, she was arguing with the Ambassador moments before he was stabbed."

Jack sighs, rubbing his temples with his hands. "Can't we have one normal event in this town?"

"No way," Maggie exclaims. "If you had normal events you wouldn't need Royal Investigators."

I laugh, sipping my latte again. Through the window, the fall wind rustles the trees, and clouds gathered overhead hint at a storm coming.

CHAPTER

Twelve

NIGHT TRANSFORMS THE CASTLE LIBRARY. Towering bookshelves lean against the walls, looking taller under the gentle golden light that emanates from a collection of lanterns strewn across the room. An All Souls Day garland of olive tree branches decorates the fireplace's mantle, perched over a crackling set of flames. Jack and I have claimed the leather chairs by the hearth, a silver tray of Chef Renauld's Halloween-themed treats balanced precariously between us. Joe stretches out at my feet, his massive body sprawled across the rug like he owns the place, which, if you ask me, he does. Beside him, Luma rests her head on his haunches, using him as a pillow.

The grandfather clock in the corner chimes eleven times, each toll reverberating through the quiet space, reminding us of the late hour. We've been talking about the case non-stop— and time always flies when I'm talking to Jack.

"You haven't tried one of these yet," Jack says, holding up what appears to be a tiny cupcake made of dark chocolate and orange ganache. "Chef Renauld outdid herself this year with the seasonal treats."

I accept the confection, biting into one end. Rich chocolate gives way to a silky pumpkin ganache center that makes me close my eyes in appreciation. "How does she make it taste like fall? It's like eating autumn."

"She's been experimenting with pumpkin spice all month." Jack reaches for a cookie shaped like a black cat, its yellow eyes made of candied lemon peel. "She brought up our wedding cake yesterday— said she'd like to be the one to make it."

The mention of our wedding sends a familiar flutter of anxiety through my chest, but I push it aside. One crisis at a time. "These ghost-shaped meringues are even better than Jocelyn's," I say, selecting one from the tray. "Don't tell her I said that, though."

Joe's ears perk up at the sound of rustling treats, his hopeful eyes tracking every movement of my hand. I break off a small piece of plain shortbread for him— the only treat Chef Renauld marked as "dog-appropriate" on her elaborate menu card.

"So," I say, brushing crumbs from my fingers onto a napkin. "Any updates on our spy theory? Has Officer Basilier found anything concrete on Missy Adeline?"

Jack's expression shifts, his eyes taking on that dark gaze that tells me he's holding back something significant. "Not exactly. But I do have news."

I straighten in my chair, immediately alert. "What kind of news?"

"I've convinced the Royal Council to reschedule the Island of Lilacs vote." He pauses, letting the words hang in the air between us. "For tomorrow morning. Here at the castle."

My mouth drops open, the ghost meringue forgotten in my hand. "Tomorrow? Here? Jack, that's—"

"Unprecedented, I know." He leans forward, his voice low despite us being alone in the vast library. "It's never been done before. Council votes are always held at the Parliament building in the capital. The Prime Minister will be enraged, that's for sure. But given the political sensitivity and the fact that we've had a murder possibly connected to the situation..."

"You thought bringing everyone involved under one roof was a good idea?" I can't keep the incredulity out of my voice. Joe senses my tension and sits up, resting his massive head on my knee. I scratch behind his ears automatically, the familiar motion helping to calm my racing thoughts.

"I can't let this vote be postponed. If the murder is connected to the vote, that's what the culprit wants," Jack says gently. "Here, we can control the environment. Officer Basilier can monitor the situation. You and Maggie can observe everyone in one place."

I take a deep breath, processing his logic. "A controlled environment. You want to set a trap?"

"Exactly. If Missy is a spy, Zacharia's evidence suggests this vote is what she's been working toward. She won't be able to resist attending. And the Prime Minister and his wife will, of course, want to be present, so you'll be able to monitor them. They're both confirmed along with representatives from Antanaro's government, various advisors, and of course, the press." Jack reaches for my hand, his warm fingers wrapping around mine. "It's our best chance to observe everyone together, to see how they interact under pressure."

"What about Ms. Labelle?" I ask, thinking of the dressmaker. "Is she invited?"

"No," Jack says, shaking his head. "It would be odd to invite her to an official state event. But if she shows up… that tells us something, doesn't it?"

"This could be dangerous," I point out. "If someone was willing to kill Ambassador Franklin over this, what's to stop them from killing again to postpone the vote?"

The firelight catches the silver in Jack's hair, highlighting his troubled expression. "Security will be tight. Officer Basilier is bringing additional officers. The castle staff has been briefed. Nothing will happen."

"You can't promise that," I say softly.

"No," he admits. "I can't. But I can promise that doing nothing— letting the vote happen elsewhere, letting our suspects scatter— means we might never solve this case. Never know who killed Franklin. Never know if I was the intended target."

Joe makes a soft whining sound, as if understanding the gravity of our conversation. I run my fingers through his thick fur, drawing strength from his solid presence.

"And if the vote passes?" I ask. "If the island is split 50/50 between Monrovia and Antanaro as planned?"

"Then we potentially remove one motive for murder," Jack says. "The island dispute will be resolved, taking away any political advantage to be gained from delaying the vote."

I reach for my tea, now lukewarm, and take a thoughtful sip. "And if it doesn't pass? If someone sways the council against the compromise?"

"Then we watch very carefully who benefits." Jack's expression turns grim. "And who seems relieved."

A log shifts in the fireplace, sending a shower of sparks up the chimney. The sudden flare of light makes the shadows leap and dance across the walls, momentarily transforming the cozy library into something more ominous.

"Who exactly will be voting?" I ask, pushing away the sense of foreboding.

"The twelve Royal Council members, plus myself as Duke. My vote is largely ceremonial—a holdover from when the monarchy had more direct power—but in the event of a tie, it becomes decisive." Jack reaches for another chocolate coffin. "The vote requires a simple majority to pass."

"And you'll vote in favor of the compromise?"

"Of course. It's the most sensible solution. Both countries

get access to the harbor and the research station. Neither loses face. And most importantly, we avoid escalating tensions."

I nod, my mind already racing ahead to tomorrow, imagining the grand council chamber filled with suspects, each with their own potential motives swirling beneath polite diplomatic smiles.

"Maggie and I will be there," I promise. "Watching everyone."

"I've already told her. She's preparing detailed dossiers on each attendee as we speak." A small smile touches Jack's lips. "I believe she canceled a date with Benjamin to do so."

"That's our Maggie," I say fondly. "Never met a crisis she couldn't organize into submission."

We fall into comfortable silence, the only sounds the crackling of the fire and Joe's occasional contented sighs. I select another treat from the tray— this one shaped like a witch's hat, dark chocolate filled with orange-infused cream.

"We'll just have to make sure nothing goes wrong tomorrow."

Jack squeezes my fingers, his smile not quite reaching his eyes. "With you and Maggie on the case? I'm sure everything will go perfectly according to plan."

But as we return to our treats and lighter conversation, I can't shake the feeling that tomorrow's vote will bring us face to face with our killer— and that when it does, not all our careful planning will be enough to keep everyone safe.

The Royal Council chamber gleams with polished splendor this morning, sunlight streaming through the tall arched windows to illuminate centuries of Monrovian history. Portraits of stern-faced ancestors watch from gilded frames as council members and dignitaries file in, their hushed conversations creating a current of anticipation that ripples through the room. Maggie and I have strategically positioned ourselves near the side entrance, where we can observe everyone without being obvious. Joe, sadly, has been relegated to the hallway outside with Luma— apparently, massive dogs are considered a diplomatic faux pas at votes that could affect international relations.

"Officer Basilier has positioned cadets at every exit," Maggie whispers, her tablet clutched against her chest like a shield. She's wearing what I've come to think of as her professional armor: a crisp navy suit with subtle gold buttons that match the royal crest. "Two plainclothes officers are seated with the press contingent."

I scan the room, noting the security precautions. "And the castle staff?"

"Only essential personnel," she confirms. "Chef Renauld is personally overseeing the refreshments to ensure no one unauthorized has access.

The massive oak table that dominates the center of the chamber has been arranged in a horseshoe configuration, thirteen ornate chairs positioned around its curve. Each place setting includes a leather portfolio containing the details of the proposed compromise, a crystal water glass, and a small Monrovian flag. At the open end of the horseshoe stands a carved wooden podium where each council member will officially cast their vote.

"Jack will open the proceedings with a ceremonial first vote," Maggie explains, following my gaze to the most elaborate chair at the center of the curve. "It's traditional for the royal representative to set the tone, though his vote only matters if there's a tie."

"He mentioned that last night," I murmur, a fresh wave of anxiety washing over me. If someone wanted to disrupt the vote or harm Jack, the moment he takes center stage would be the perfect opportunity.

The chamber doors swing open, and a hush falls as Prime

Minister Floridán enters, his impressive mustache seeming extra bristly this morning. He's wearing a dark suit with a yellow tie— not the same shade as our murder fabric, I note with relief, but a more subdued gold that matches the Monrovian flag. My eyes scan the space behind him, but there's no sign of his wife.

"Where's Ginevière?" I whisper to Maggie, who's already tapping on her tablet.

"According to her assistant, she's feeling unwell this morning," Maggie reports, her eyebrows lifting in skepticism. "Convenient timing, isn't it?"

Before I can respond, Missy Adeline makes her entrance, and "entrance" is definitely the right word. She sweeps into the room wearing a tailored red suit that somehow manages to be both appropriate for a political proceeding and utterly eye-catching. Every head turns to watch her progress to the visitors' gallery, where she takes a seat in the front row, directly in my line of sight.

I scan the faces around her, searching for her ever-present shadow. "No sign of Sacks," I observe.

"He was spotted leaving the village early this morning," Maggie confirms. "Claimed he had an emergency meeting with a client in the capital."

"Another convenient absence," I mutter, my suspicions ratcheting up several notches. "Maybe we should tell Officer Basilier—"

The announcement of Jack's arrival cuts me off. He enters from a side door, looking every inch the Duke in his formal attire, though I can see the tension in his shoulders that others would miss. His eyes meet mine briefly as he takes his place, and I try to communicate reassurance with my gaze alone.

"All rise for the Royal Council of Monrovia," intones a uniformed official.

The twelve council members process in, each wearing the traditional blue sash of office across their formal attire. They take their places around the table with practiced dignity, arranging their portfolios and adjusting their chairs with the synchronized movements of people who have performed this ritual countless times before.

Officer Basilier slips in through the side entrance, positioning herself against the wall near us. Her sharp eyes continuously scan the room, one hand resting near her hip where I know her service weapon is holstered.

"Missing suspects?" she asks under her breath, not looking at us.

"Two," Maggie confirms just as quietly. "Sacks and Geneviève Floridán. Technically three, if you count Ms. Labelle, but she was not invited in the first place. It would have said more if she'd shown up."

Officer Basilier nods almost imperceptibly. "Noted."

The council chair, a distinguished woman with silver hair twisted into an elegant knot, calls the session to order. "We gather today for an extraordinary session of the Royal Council to vote on the proposed compromise regarding Île des Lilas," she announces, her voice carrying easily through the chamber without seeming loud. "As per tradition, His Grace the Duke of Atwood will cast the first vote, which will become a tie breaker should the other votes yield a fifty percent split."

Jack rises from his seat, the picture of royal dignity. As he moves toward the podium, I can't help but feel a surge of pride mixed with anxiety. He stands tall, confident in his role despite the danger we suspect might be lurking.

"Before I cast my vote," Jack begins, his voice steady and clear, "I want to acknowledge the importance of this moment. The compromise before us represents not just a resolution to a territorial dispute, but an opportunity for Monrovia and Antanaro to demonstrate that cooperation is possible even in the face of—"

A sharp crack interrupts him— so loud it seems to physically strike the air. For one frozen moment, nothing happens. Then a collective gasp rises as the massive crystal chandelier directly above the voting podium sways violently, the chains securing it to the ceiling groaning under stress.

"Jack!" I scream, my body moving before my mind can fully process what's happening. I lunge forward just as the chandelier tears free, its enormous weight plummeting toward where Jack stands.

Time slows impossibly. I see Jack dive sideways, his reflexes saving him from being directly crushed. The chandelier crashes onto the podium with a deafening explosion of crystal and metal, sending deadly shards flying in all directions. Screams erupt throughout the chamber as council members and visitors scramble for the exits.

I reach Jack just as he's pushing himself up with one arm, the other held awkwardly against his chest. Blood seeps through the sleeve of his jacket, but his eyes are clear and focused when they meet mine.

"I'm alright," he says immediately, though the tightness around his mouth tells me he's in pain. "Just caught some debris."

"Don't move," I instruct, already shrugging off my jacket to press against the bleeding spot on his arm. Over my shoulder, I can see Maggie has taken charge of the evacuation, her voice rising above the chaos with remarkable authority as she directs people toward the exits.

Officer Basilier pushes through the panicked crowd, barking orders to her cadets as she makes her way to us. "Secure the room! No one leaves without being checked!" She kneels beside us, her eyes quickly assessing Jack's injury. "How bad?"

"I don't think it's deep," I say, lifting my jacket slightly to check. "Looks like a laceration from flying glass, not a puncture."

"Medical team is on the way," she assures us, before

turning her attention to the destroyed chandelier. She circles it carefully, her experienced eyes taking in details I would miss.

"The chain," she says after a moment, pointing to the ceiling where the chandelier had hung. "Look at the end."

I follow her gaze, noting the clean, even edge of the metal links where they've separated from the ceiling mount.

"That's not metal fatigue," Officer Basilier states flatly. "That's a deliberate cut, made with bolt cutters or something similar." She turns back to us, her expression grim. "This wasn't an accident."

Jack's eyes meet mine, a silent confirmation passing between us. Someone tried to kill him— right here, in front of dozens of witnesses, at the exact moment he was about to publicly support the island compromise.

"The missing suspects," I say urgently to Officer Basilier. "Sacks and Ginevière—"

"Already on it," she confirms, pulling out her radio. "I've ordered roadblocks at all routes out of Monrovia. If they're involved, they won't get far."

Maggie returns to our side, the chamber now emptied except for security personnel and medical staff hurrying through the door. "Everyone's in the great hall being processed," she reports. "I've locked down the castle. No one in or out."

As the medical team takes over caring for Jack's injury, I step back, surveying the destruction. Crystal shards glitter across the ancient wooden floor like malevolent stars, the ornate podium crushed beyond recognition beneath the chandelier's massive frame. Where Jack had been standing just moments ago, a large metal spike from the chandelier's central post now protrudes vertically—a deadly spear that would have impaled him if he hadn't moved.

"That was meant for you," I say quietly when the medical team gives me space to approach Jack again.

He nods, wincing slightly as the medic wraps his arm.

"Whoever did this doesn't care about subtlety anymore. They're getting desperate."

"And desperate people make mistakes," Officer Basilier adds, joining our huddle. "The security cameras in this room were disabled, but the ones in the corridors were functioning. We'll find who did this."

I look around at the shattered crystal, the destroyed podium, the bloodstains on the ancient floor, and feel a cold determination settling in my chest. This isn't just about solving a murder anymore. Someone tried to kill Jack—*my Jack*—in front of my eyes.

"Yes," I agree, my voice steadier than I feel inside. "We will."

CHAPTER
Thirteen

THE ANTISEPTIC SMELL of the hospital fills my nostrils as I watch the doctor suture Jack's arm. Sixteen stitches so far and counting. I keep my face neutral, but inside I'm cycling between fury and terror. Someone tried to kill Jack today—right in front of me, right in the heart of what was supposed to be the safest place in Monrovia. I squeeze Joe's leash a little tighter, and he leans his massive body against my leg, a warm, furry reminder that we're all still here, still breathing.

I remember the last time I was in the hospital and how upset Jack was. *Now, I understand how he felt.*

"You don't have to watch this," Jack says, noticing my fixed gaze on the needle weaving through his skin. Despite everything, his voice remains steady. Royal training, I suppose—dukes don't wince during medical procedures.

"I'm fine," I lie, forcing myself to look directly at the wound. The laceration runs from just below his elbow halfway to his wrist, a jagged line where flying crystal from the shattered chandelier sliced through his jacket and into flesh. It could have been so much worse. Six inches to the left and it would have caught his neck instead of his arm. I swallow hard against the thought.

"Almost done, Your Grace," the doctor murmurs, tying off another stitch with practiced fingers. "You're very fortunate. The cut is clean and missed any major blood vessels or tendons."

"Lucky me," Jack says with a wry smile that doesn't quite reach his eyes. "I'm mangled just in time for wedding season."

I try to return his smile but can't quite manage it. The image of the chandelier crashing down, the deadly metal spike that would have impaled him if he hadn't moved— it's all too fresh, too vivid. I feel Joe shift against my leg again, as if he senses my distress and is trying to ground me.

Maggie stands near the door, her tablet clutched to her chest like armor, while Luma sits obediently at her feet. Somehow, Maggie managed to get both dogs into the hospital despite strict "no animals" policies. I suspect she invoked some obscure royal privilege or, more likely, simply bulldozed through objections with her particular brand of polite insistence that leaves no room for argument.

"Officer Basilier called," she informs us, her voice low. "Security footage shows someone entering the council chamber at 4:30 this morning, before the guards changed shifts. They're enhancing the images now."

"And the roadblocks?" Jack asks, not flinching as the doctor begins work on the final stitches.

"No sign of Sacks or Geneviève yet," Maggie says, her expression tight with concern. "But the Police are trying to locate them both now."

The doctor finishes the last stitch— twenty-two in total— and begins cleaning the area around the wound. "I'll bandage this now, Your Grace. You'll need to keep it dry for at least 48 hours, and I'm prescribing antibiotics as a precaution. The stitches can come out in ten days."

Jack nods, his eyes finding mine across the small examination room. Despite everything, I see a flicker of humor there that makes my heart swell. Even with blood on his shirt and his arm sliced open, he's still Jack— *my* Jack— who somehow finds reasons to smile in the midst of chaos.

Once the doctor finishes the bandaging and leaves us with care instructions, a nurse brings in extra chairs so we can all sit comfortably around Jack's bed. For a few minutes, no one speaks. Joe settles at my feet, his massive head resting on my shoes, while Luma circles three times before curling up beside Maggie's chair.

"So," Jack finally breaks the silence, "I think we can safely cross 'falling chandelier' off our list of potential wedding decorations."

The tension breaks. Maggie lets out a surprised snort of laughter, and I feel my own lips twitch despite myself.

"I was thinking more along the lines of fairy lights anyway," I play along, reaching for his uninjured hand. "Less lethal."

"A wise choice," Jack agrees, his fingers intertwining with mine. "Though I must say, if someone wanted to stop the vote, they've succeeded. The council members scattered like startled pigeons."

"The vote will be rescheduled," Maggie assures him. "And next time, we'll have the council chamber swept for tampering beforehand."

I shake my head, still struggling to process everything that's happened. "I can't believe someone would go this far. A public assassination attempt, in front of dozens of witnesses?"

"It suggests desperation," Jack says thoughtfully. "Or extreme confidence in their ability to escape undetected."

"Or both," Maggie adds, her fingers tapping against her tablet as if itching to take notes.

Joe makes a soft huffing sound from the floor, lifting his head to gaze at Jack with what I swear is concern in his doggy eyes. Jack notices and smiles, reaching down with his good arm to scratch behind Joe's ears.

"I'm okay, big guy," he tells my dog. "It'll take more than a falling light fixture to get rid of me."

"This is getting to be a habit, though," I say, thinking of all the times one or both of us has ended up in a hospital or emergency situation over the past year. "We really need to find less dramatic hobbies."

"Like what?" Jack asks, amusement dancing in his eyes despite the circumstances. "Knitting? Birdwatching?"

"I was thinking more along the lines of competitive napping," I suggest. "Or professional staying-away-from-murderers."

"You'd be terrible at both," Maggie points out with fond exasperation. "Especially the second one."

"She's right," Jack says, squeezing my hand. "You have a particular talent for finding trouble."

"Me?" I protest. "I'm not the one who just had a chandelier dropped on them!"

"Technically, it missed me," Jack corrects, then winces as he accidentally moves his injured arm. "Mostly."

We all fall silent again, the reality of how close we came to tragedy settling over us once more. I watch Jack's face, memorizing every line, every angle, overwhelmed by the knowledge that I could have lost him today.

"At least it's just the hospital this time," Maggie says after a moment, her voice deliberately light. "And not, you know, prison."

"Personally," Jack says, adjusting his hospital gown with an air of dignity, "I think I prefer prison to hospitals. The food is better."

I offer a meek laugh but wish we could change the subject. The weight of what my investigations has brought down upon the group of people I love suddenly feels very heavy.

As if reading my thoughts, Jack turns to Maggie. "Would you mind giving Rebecca and me a moment? And perhaps taking the dogs for a quick walk? I imagine they could use a break."

"Of course," Maggie says, immediately understanding. She stands, gathering both leashes. "Come on, you two. Let's go find some grass to sniff."

Joe looks at me, clearly reluctant to leave my side after the day's events. "It's okay, buddy," I assure him. "We'll be right here."

With a resigned huff, he follows Maggie and Luma from the room, casting one last concerned glance at Jack before the door closes behind them.

Alone at last, the hospital room feels suddenly smaller, more intimate. Jack shifts on the bed, wincing slightly as he adjusts his position to face me more directly.

"Rebecca," he begins, his voice softer now that it's just the two of us. "I need to tell you something."

"I know," I say, sure that Jack is going to say what I'm thinking. "The Royal Investigators have to stop. It's brought nothing but trouble to you, me, and Maggie. One of us is always getting arrested or hospitalized and it's all my fault and—"

"What?" Jack says, blinking away the surprise in his eyes. "My goodness, of course you can't stop the Royal Investigators. Look at how much good you've done."

"Oh," I answer, reeling. "Then, you were talking about…"

"Not about the investigation," he says gently. "It's about us. About our wedding."

My heart does a little stutter-step in my chest. With everything that's happened, our ongoing wedding debate had temporarily faded into the background of my concerns. "What about it?"

Jack takes a deep breath, his eyes holding mine with an intensity that makes my breath catch. "When that chandelier was falling— in that split second when I realized what was happening— do you know what I thought about?"

I shake my head silently.

"You," he says simply. "Not the vote, not the kingdom, not my duty to Monrovia. Just you, and the life we're building together, and how desperately I wanted more time with you." His uninjured hand finds mine again, holding tight. "And I realized something important."

"What?" I ask, my voice barely above a whisper.

"I've been trying too hard to give Monrovia everything," he admits, a shadow passing across his face. "To be the perfect Duke, to make up for years when I wasn't. Opening the castle, the animal sanctuary, the community initiatives— they're all important, and I don't regret any of them. But our wedding?" He shakes his head. "I've been pushing for something grand and public because I thought that's what was expected, what the people deserved. And today, that same attitude nearly cost me my life."

"Jack—"

"Let me finish," he says gently. "When I was lying there, with glass all around me and my arm bleeding, all I could think was how ridiculous it was to argue about wedding details when what matters— the only thing that truly matters — is that we're together." His voice catches slightly. "I don't want a royal spectacle, Rebecca. I never have. I've just been trying to do what I thought was right for everyone else."

I feel tears pricking at the corners of my eyes, overwhelmed by his words and the emotion behind them. "What are you saying?"

"I'm saying I want a small wedding," Jack declares, his voice stronger now, more certain. "Just us and the people we truly care about. Somewhere peaceful and beautiful." A smile touches his lips. "Somewhere with giraffes, perhaps."

A laugh bubbles up through my tears. "Giraffe? Specifically?"

"Well, Alfredo would be terribly offended if he wasn't invited, don't you think?" Jack's eyes are twinkling now.

"And I happen to know the caretaker of a certain animal sanctuary who might be willing to host a very private ceremony."

"You want to get married at the sanctuary?" I clarify, my heart swelling at the thought.

"I want to marry you," Jack emphasizes, bringing my hand to his lips for a gentle kiss. "In a place that represents who we are together, not just our titles or positions. A place where we both feel at home."

I think about the sanctuary— our peaceful refuge away from royal duties and public scrutiny, where Jack reads poetry to the alpacas and I've taught Alfredo to take treats from visitors' hands. Where Joe can run free without a leash and Luma can herd imaginary flocks to her heart's content.

"It sounds perfect," I whisper, leaning forward to kiss him softly, mindful of his injury. "Absolutely perfect."

When we break apart, Jack's smile is brighter than I've seen it in weeks, the weight of expectation visibly lifting from his shoulders despite the bandages and hospital gown. "The Queen will be disappointed," he acknowledges with a small shrug that suggests he's made peace with this fact.

"We'll invite her," I offer generously. "She can watch Alfredo eat pasta while we say our vows."

"An experience no royal wedding has ever offered before," Jack laughs, then grimaces as the movement jostles his arm. "Pioneering new traditions, that's us."

I lean forward, resting my forehead gently against his. "I love you, Jack. I'd marry you anywhere— castle, sanctuary, hospital room— as long as we're together."

"I'll marry you anywhere," Jack answers, "… as long as it's a place without chandeliers."

"I'll hold you to that," I say, kissing him again just as the door opens to readmit Maggie and the dogs.

Joe immediately bounds over to check on us, his massive tail wagging with relief when he sees we're both intact and smiling. Luma follows more sedately, but her eyes are bright with the same canine concern.

"Everything okay?" Maggie asks, taking in our clasped hands and suspiciously damp eyes.

"Better than okay," I tell her, unable to keep the smile from my face. "We've finally decided on our wedding plans."

"Thank goodness," Maggie exhales dramatically. "I was beginning to think I'd have to plan the whole thing myself just to get it done before we're all too old to walk down the aisle."

"Well, you'll still have plenty to do," Jack informs her. "But perhaps a bit less than you anticipated."

"We're keeping it small," I explain. "At the sanctuary. Just family and close friends."

"And giraffes," Jack adds solemnly. "Can't forget the giraffes."

Maggie blinks twice, processing this information, then breaks into a wide smile. "It's perfect," she declares, already reaching for her tablet. "I'll start a new planning document immediately. 'Royal Wedding: Safari Edition.'"

As she begins tapping away, already lost in logistics, Jack catches my eye and winks. In the midst of danger and uncertainty, with a killer still at large and questions still unanswered, we've found our way to one important truth: when everything else falls apart—sometimes literally— what matters most is being true to ourselves and to each other.

And if that means saying "I do" while Alfredo the giraffe watches with mild interest, well, that's exactly the kind of wedding I've always wanted.

CHAPTER
Fourteen

"OKAY," I say, looking into the entrance of *Café de Flore*. "Jocelyn has officially gone too far."

I motion toward the café, which is filled to the brim with decor that reflects the spirit of Halloween. Every time we've stopped by, Jocelyn has added something new, but now— the café looks more like a Halloween store than a place to grab a lavender latte. Orange flowers are arranged on the walls in a giant mural, and black bats dangle from the ceiling. Pumpkins leer in an explosion of orange, and an actual cauldron bubbles in the corner, emitting some kind of purple smoke. It's too much. Joe freezes at the entrance, looking at me like I've led him into a festive nightmare realm.

"There's still pancakes inside, buddy," I assure him. "And I'm sure Jocelyn has some for you." The word "pancakes" is all it takes to get Joe moving. He gives me a deeply skeptical look but then pads across the threshold, his nails clicking against the wooden floor as he maneuvers around a life-sized witch figure that cackles when we pass.

The ceiling has disappeared beneath a canopy of fake cobwebs interwoven with tiny orange lights. The usual scent of coffee and pastries now competes with cinnamon, clove, and something mysteriously herbal that wafts from the smoking cauldron.

"Rebecca! Over here!" Maggie waves from our usual corner table, which now sits beneath what appears to be a full-sized papier-mâché cemetery arch. Officer Basilier sits across from her, looking distinctly uncomfortable as a motion-activated ghost periodically moans above her head.

I navigate through the Halloween labyrinth, dodging animated ravens and steering Joe away from a display of realistic-looking eyeballs floating in glass jars. "This is... something," I manage as I reach their table, unwinding my scarf and draping it over a chair that's been painted to look like it's made of bones.

"Jocelyn says it's her 'modest tribute' to All Souls Day," Maggie informs me, her face perfectly serious though her eyes sparkle with amusement. "Apparently last year was just a 'soft launch' of her vision. She's really gone all out this time." Maggie leans in, whispering, "I heard a rumor she was dating someone and just broke up with him. Seems like she's pouring her all into decorating. Do you think she's okay?"

"Uhm," I say, looking around the packed café. "I'm going to go with… no."

"I'm worried about fire hazards," Officer Basilier mutters, eyeing a cluster of (thankfully battery-operated) candles nestled among artificial autumn leaves. "And sanitation. Are those *real* pumpkins hanging from the ceiling?"

I glance up. Indeed, dozens of miniature pumpkins dangle above us, each carved with intricate designs that cast spooky patterns across the tables when the lights inside them flicker.

"I think they've been preserved somehow," Maggie says. "Jocelyn mentioned something about a special solution that keeps them from rotting. She was talking so fast when she told me about the decorations I barely caught what she said!"

Joe settles himself under the table with a heavy sigh, his massive head resting on my feet. I notice he's carefully positioned himself as far as possible from a grinning skeleton dog that sits near the counter, wearing a spiked collar and holding a sign that says "Bone Appetit" in dripping red letters.

"Good call, Joe," I murmur, patting his side with my foot. "That thing is definitely cursed."

Jocelyn appears at our table as if summoned by our discussion of her decorations, gliding through her spooky café . She's wearing a flowing black dress, in contrast to her usually quiet demeanor, and her brown hair is threaded with tiny orange and black ribbons.

"Welcome back!" she says warmly, her voice barely rising above the ambient sounds of moaning ghosts and cackling witches. "I've prepared special treats for today. Perhaps you'd like to try our Witch's Brew lattes? They're made with acti-vated charcoal and cinnamon, topped with orange-tinted whipped cream."

"That sounds..." I search for a diplomatic word, "memorable."

"I'll have one," Maggie says brightly. "And maybe those bat-shaped cookies you have in the display case?"

"Regular coffee, black," Officer Basilier says firmly. "No charcoal, no whipped cream, no... activation."

"I'll try the Witch's Brew," I decide, figuring I might as well embrace the madness. "And whatever pastry is least likely to give me nightmares."

"Our pumpkin soul cakes are quite peaceful," Jocelyn assures me with complete seriousness. "And for Joe, perhaps a ghost-shaped biscuit? They're flavored with peanut butter and a touch of carob."

Joe perks up at the mention of peanut butter, his earlier wariness forgotten.

"Sure," I agree!

"Coming up!" Jocelyn smiles brightly, then sighs. "Don't you just love this time of year? It's a reminder that anything is possible!"

I smile and nod, and Jocelyn glides away, disappearing behind a curtain of hanging cobwebs. In no time at all, she returns with our drinks. My Witch's Brew is indeed an alarming shade of black with neon orange whipped cream swirled on top. Officer Basilier's plain black coffee somehow looks even more ominous by comparison— a void of normalcy in a sea of Halloween excess.

"Your soul cakes," Jocelyn says, placing a plate before me. The pastries are round and golden, stamped with intricate symbols. "Traditionally, they were given to revelers who would pray for the dead. Each symbol represents a different blessing for the departed."

"That's... informative," I say, wondering what exactly I'm about to eat. "Thank you."

"And for Joe." She bends down to place a large ghost-shaped biscuit on the floor beside him. Joe sniffs it cautiously before taking it gently between his massive jaws.

As Jocelyn moves away to help another customer— a young couple who look equal parts delighted and terrified by the decor— Officer Basilier leans forward, her expression shifting from mild discomfort to deadly seriousness.

"I have news," she says, her voice dropping to just above a whisper. "About the chandelier incident."

Maggie and I instantly forget about the Halloween madness surrounding us, our attention snapping to Basilier's face.

"The security logs?" Maggie prompts, already reaching for her tablet.

Basilier nods, taking a sip of her plain coffee as if drawing strength from its normalcy. "We've been reviewing all footage from the castle. Ten minutes before the chandelier fell, someone entered the restricted gallery mezzanine—the area directly above the council chamber with access to the chandelier's mounting hardware."

My heart beats faster. "You have them on camera? Who was it?"

"That's the thing," Basilier says, frustration evident in her voice. "They kept their face turned away from the cameras, wore a maintenance uniform with the collar up. But—" she pauses, placing her coffee down with deliberate care, "we can estimate their height from the video. The person is on the shorter side. Around 5'7" or 5'6"."

"That could be either Sacks or Geneviève," I think out loud. "They're both on the shorter side. You really can't see the person's face in the video?"

Officer Basilier shakes her head. "No. They had a hat on their head… a mask covering their lower face. There's no way to identify them."

"We know that Missy Adeline and the Prime Minister were both present during the vote count," Maggie says thoughtfully. "Which means only three of our suspects could have had time to rig the chandelier to fall. Sacks. The Prime Minister's wife, Geneviève. Or Ms. Labelle."

The overhead lights flicker suddenly, making all three of us tense. A moment later, Jocelyn's voice calls out apologetically from behind the counter: "Sorry! Just testing the new spooky light effect for tonight's ghost story reading!"

I exhale slowly, realizing how on edge we all are. Even Joe rose to alert status, his head up and ears forward until he determines there's no threat.

"What's our next move?" I ask Basilier, pushing my half-finished Witch's Brew aside. The novelty has worn off, leaving only a strange charcoal aftertaste.

"We've found Sacks and Geneviève," Officer Basilier answers. "I've had my officers interview them both, and they each claimed they had nothing to do with the chandelier."

"What were their reasons for not attending the vote?"

"Sacks claimed he had an important work phone call," Officer Basilier rolls her eyes. "I can't imagine anything that man does is actually important, but we were able to verify the call with his office. And Geneviève claimed she was home sick. She did appear to be sniffling, according to my officers, and they were able to verify a prescription for cough medicine filled at the local pharmacy."

"What about Ms. Labelle?" I ask.

"She was allegedly at her dress shop at the time, although she couldn't provide the names of any customers who came by."

"I still don't understand something," Maggie says, tapping her tablet thoughtfully. "If the killer was after Ambassador Franklin, why strike again?"

"Desperation," I suggest. "Maybe they killed to try and delay the vote. And when that failed, they decided to kill again."

"I think this confirms that our killer is, in fact, trying to stop the vote about the island," Basilier says, her expression darkening.

Joe nudges my hand with his nose, sensing my unease. I scratch behind his ears automatically, the familiar texture of his fur comforting against my fingertips.

"We're getting closer," I say more to myself than anyone else. My brain runs in circles—there's something about this case I'm missing. Something simple that will give us the answer we seek. "We'll keep working on it."

Basilier nods, already standing and dropping money on the table for our Halloween monstrosities. "Stay in touch. And Orange—" her eyes meet mine, uncharacteristic concern visible beneath her professional demeanor, "be careful. You're a public figure now. The killer wasn't able to get to the Duke, and he… or *she*… might decide you're the next best target."

"Charming thought," I mutter, but I know she's right. "Don't worry. I've got my four-legged security detail." I pat Joe's side, and he rises to his feet, massive and alert beside me.

As we navigate back through Jocelyn's Halloween wonderland toward the exit, ducking under swooping bats and sidestepping animated skeletons, I can't shake the feeling that the café's playful spookiness is a poor imitation of the real dangers waiting for us outside. Someone cut a chandelier chain in an attempt to kill my fiancé. Someone killed Ambassador Franklin. And now, that someone is still out there, pursuing goals we don't fully understand.

"Rebecca," Maggie says as we step outside into the crisp autumn air, Joe padding heavily beside us, "what if we've been looking at this all wrong?"

I pause on the cobblestone street, turning to face her. "What do you mean?"

Her expression is troubled, her usual efficiency momentarily replaced by uncertainty. "I don't know exactly. It just feels like we're missing something. We keep looking at each person individually, but I feel like there's more to it. I'm not sure why I just—"

"I know," I tell her. "We're missing something."

Joe looks up at me, his wise eyes seeming to reflect the same concern. And as the wind carries the sound of Jocelyn's mechanical witches laughing from inside the café, I can't help but agree. We're missing something important— something that makes killing Ambassador Franklin and trying to kill Jack worth the risk.

And I have a feeling that when we finally discover what it is, we'll wish we'd stayed surrounded by Jocelyn's fake monsters rather than facing the real ones waiting for us.

THE LIGHT from my apartment's lamp catches in Jack's hair, turning the salt-and-pepper strands into something magical. Joe and Luma are playing with a water bottle— the latest treasure Luma made from trash after raiding my recycle bin.

"More tea?" I ask, reaching for the delicate porcelain pot Chef Renauld sent up with our evening snack. The spicy-sweet aroma of pumpkin and cinnamon wafts through my apartment, making the space feel even cozier than it already is.

"Please," Jack says, extending his cup with his good arm. His other arm remains wrapped in a pristine white bandage, a stark reminder of how close I came to losing him.

I pour carefully, watching the amber liquid steam in the cool evening air. "How's the arm feeling?"

"Better," he says, but I catch the slight wince as he shifts position. "Renauld's been sending up those pain-relieving herbal teas along with the pumpkin. I think she's trying to drug me into submission so I'll stay in bed longer."

"Smart woman," I mutter, setting the teapot down. "Remind me to thank her."

Jack smiles his most crooked grin. "If I listened to everyone telling me to rest, I'd never get anything done."

At our feet, Joe lets out a dramatic sigh and rolls onto his back, all 250 pounds of him somehow convinced he's a lapdog. Luma, more reasonably sized but no less dramatic, immediately repositions herself to drape across his belly. They've become an unlikely pair— my enormous, golden Tibetan Mastiff and Jack's elegant collie.

"Your dog is corrupting mine," Jack observes, watching Luma bat at Joe's tail.

Luma, hearing herself discussed, perks up her ears and gives us her most innocent expression.

Jack laughs, then winces again, his hand moving instinctively to his bandaged arm. I pretend not to notice, but my chest tightens. The image of him lying beneath that massive chandelier flashes through my mind— the dust, the blood, the absolute terror that had gripped me.

"You know," I say, trying to keep my voice casual, "no one would blame you if you postponed the vote for a few more days. A week, even."

Jack takes a sip of his tea, his eyes studying me over the rim of his cup. "Rebecca," he says, setting the cup down gently. "We've talked about this."

That didn't count as talking, I think, shaking my head. When we sat down for tea, Jack told me he had rescheduled the vote on the island for tomorrow in the Village Square. I was in such shock I froze, and Jack quickly moved on to other subjects. I haven't argued with him yet, but I'm gearing up for it now.

"I know, I know. It's just—" I hesitate, searching for the right words. "Someone tried to *kill* you, Jack. They dropped a chandelier on you during a royal vote. That's not exactly subtle."

Jack reaches over with his good hand and takes mine. His palm is warm from the teacup, his fingers strong as they curl around mine. "I have a responsibility to move forward with the Island of Lilacs negotiations. Too much is at stake."

I sigh, knowing he's right but hating it all the same.

"At least the vote tomorrow will be in the Village Square," Jack continues, squeezing my hand. "Public, open, with plenty of witnesses. No chandeliers to worry about."

"Just snipers," I mutter darkly, immediately regretting it when I see the flash of concern cross his face. "Sorry. Professional hazard. I spent too many years doing threat assessments for the safari park."

"Your paranoia is one of your most charming qualities," Jack says dryly, but his eyes are kind. "It's what makes you such an excellent detective."

"Former animal trainer turned amateur detective," I correct him. "And my 'paranoia' has saved your royal self more than once."

"Which is why I listen when you have specific concerns," he counters. "But this vote needs to happen, Rebecca. The longer we delay, the more opportunity for the opposition to organize."

I know he's right. I just hate the feeling of playing catch-up with whoever killed Ambassador Franklin and tried to take out Jack. I feel like I'm behind— like I'm missing something important about this case— and it's bothering me.

Joe must sense my anxiety because he rolls to his feet and pads over, resting his massive head on my knee. I sink my fingers into his thick golden fur, drawing comfort from his solid presence.

"I'll be there tomorrow," I tell Jack, meeting his eyes directly. "Front row, with Joe."

"I would expect nothing less." His lips quirk up in that half-smile that makes him look younger than his forty-something years. "You know, you're quite the inspiration."

I snort inelegantly. "Right. Woman who talks to animals and stumbles over murderers. Very inspiring."

"I mean it." His voice turns serious. "You never back down when things get dangerous. When you started Royal Investigations with Maggie, half the village thought it was a joke. Now you're solving crimes the Royal Guard couldn't crack. You keep going, no matter what."

Heat rises to my cheeks. Even after months together, I'm still not used to Jack's earnest compliments. "That's different," I mumble.

"Is it? You face danger head-on because you believe in justice. That's why I'm facing tomorrow's vote for the same reason—because I believe in what we're trying to accomplish for both countries."

I can't argue with his logic, but that doesn't mean I have to like it. "Fine. But promise me you'll stay alert. And let the Royal Guard do their jobs."

"Promise," he says solemnly, then ruins the effect with a quick kiss to my knuckles. "Besides, there's safety in numbers. The entire village council will be there, along with representatives from Antanaro. Even the press."

Something about his words catches in my mind like a burr. Safety in numbers. The phrase echoes, triggering some half-formed connection that I can't quite grasp.

"Rebecca?" Jack's voice seems distant suddenly. "Did I lose you?"

"Safety in numbers," I repeat slowly. "That's... interesting."

"What is?" He looks genuinely puzzled.

I shake my head, trying to chase down the thought. "I'm not sure yet. Something about that phrase..."

Joe lifts his head, sensing my change in mood. His dark eyes fix on me with that uncanny perception that sometimes makes me wonder if he understands every word we say.

"It's nothing," I say, but we both know that's not true. My brain is already sorting through evidence, statements, time-lines— trying to connect whatever just sparked in my subconscious to Ambassador Franklin's murder and the chandelier incident.

"It's never nothing with you," Jack says with a mix of fondness and resignation. "I can practically see the gears turning."

I give him an apologetic smile. "Occupational hazard. Just like your diplomatic non-answers and royal wave."

"I do not have a royal wave," he protests, demonstrating exactly that with his uninjured arm.

Safety in numbers. Why does it feel significant?

"You're still thinking about it," Jack observes, interrupting my thoughts.

"Sorry." I try to refocus on him, on this moment. The soft lamplight, our dogs at our feet, the tea growing cold on the table. "I'll sleep on it," I say. "The answer will come to me."

We lapse into comfortable silence, but my mind keeps turning over that phrase. *Safety in numbers.* The killer uses crowds as cover. They strike when surrounded by people, when their target feels secure. Which means tomorrow's public vote in the Village Square isn't the safe option Jack thinks it is—it might be exactly what our murderer is counting on.

I don't say this aloud, not wanting to worry Jack further when he's already made up his mind. Instead, I nestle closer to him on the couch, my brain cataloging precautions, mapping sightlines, planning security measures. If the killer wants to use the crowd as cover tomorrow, they'll have to get past me, Joe, Maggie, and the entire Royal Guard first.

Safety in numbers. The phrase continues to echo as the evening grows later, as Jack reluctantly returns to his royal quarters, as I prepare for bed with Joe standing guard by my door. It follows me into my dreams, where faceless figures move through crowds, hands concealing weapons, eyes fixed on unsuspecting targets.

Safety in numbers. But for whom?

CHAPTER
Sixteen

THE TOWN SQUARE has transformed itself into a glorious celebration of All Souls Day. Marigold garlands drape from lampposts to trees, their vibrant orange a defiant shout against the approaching winter. Candles flicker in windowsills, on makeshift altars, and along the edges of the newly constructed platform where the Royal Council will soon cast their votes on the fate of Île des Lilas. Joe presses against my leg, his massive body a comforting weight as we stand at the edge of the gathering crowd. His ears prick forward, sensing the same electric tension that makes my own skin prickle. This isn't just a vote anymore— it's a reckoning.

"They've really outdone themselves," Maggie murmurs beside me, her tablet clutched to her chest like a shield. She's wearing her most formal outfit— a structured navy blazer with the royal crest subtly embroidered on the pocket— but has conceded to the holiday with a small pumpkin pinned to her lapel.

"Jocelyn would approve," I agree, taking in the paper skeletons dancing from strings attached to the gazebo, the elaborate sugar skulls adorning the refreshment tables, and the hundreds of flickering candles creating islands of golden light in the deepening dusk.

The square is packed, and I'm once again unsure if Jack's idea to hold the vote in the Village Square was a good one. My eyes scan the crowd, mentally checking off suspects like I'm taking attendance. Ms. Labelle stands near her shop, looking nervous but elegant in a simple black dress. The Prime Minister occupies a prominent position near the platform, his impressive mustache twitching with barely contained impatience. Beside him stands his wife, Ginevière, looking as if she's fully recovered from her alleged flu.

"There's Missy," Maggie whispers, subtly tilting her head toward the refreshment table.

Sure enough, Missy Adeline holds court near the mulled wine, a vision in emerald green that somehow manages to be both festive and formal. She laughs at something someone says, the sound carrying across the square with practiced musicality. Sacks hovers at her elbow, his signature paisley bow tie seeming particularly garish against the holiday decorations. His eyes dart around the square with the nervous energy of a cornered animal.

"And there's Jack," I breathe.

He stands at the edge of the platform, speaking with the Royal Council Chair. His left arm remains in a sling, the white bandage visible beneath his rolled-up sleeve, but he's otherwise impeccable in a charcoal suit that makes him look both regal and approachable. As if sensing my gaze, he looks up, his eyes finding mine across the crowd. A smile breaks across his face— the private one, just for me, that crinkles the corners of his eyes and makes him look younger, less burdened by duty.

"Go," Maggie says, giving me a gentle push. "You've got about ten minutes before the ceremony starts. Our killer is here, and I can't wait to see their expression when it all comes crashing down."

I weave through the crowd, Joe creating a natural path as people instinctively make way for his massive bulk. When I reach Jack, he pulls me close with his good arm.

"You're supposed to be resting," I scold, though I can't keep the relief from my voice.

"I'm standing still and looking important," he counters. "That's practically the definition of rest for a duke."

"How's the arm?" I ask, gently touching the edge of his sling.

"Hurts like hell," he admits quietly, for my ears only. "But I wasn't about to miss this." His eyes search my face. "Are you sure about this plan? Once you start, there's no going back."

Late last night, I woke up in the middle of sleep, understanding what I had to do. The answer struck me out of nowhere, and it was all because of what Jack said:

There's safety in numbers.

I nod, feeling a strange calm settle over me. For the past twenty-four hours, Maggie, Officer Basilier, and I have been piecing together the final threads of evidence, connecting dots we should have seen earlier. "It has to be now, with everyone present. We might not get another chance."

Jack nods, his expression turning serious. "The Council is ready whenever you are. I've explained that there's a security matter to address before the vote." His fingers intertwine with mine, squeezing gently. "Be careful, Rebecca."

A soft bell rings, signaling the start of the ceremony. Jack squeezes my hand once more before releasing it, moving to take his position on the platform. I return to Maggie's side, where Officer Basilier has now joined us, her uniform crisp and her expression guarded.

"Everyone in position?" I ask her quietly.

She nods. "Officers at every exit. Plainclothes among the crowd. Roadblocks on all routes out of the village." She hands me a small microphone. "Clip this to your collar. It'll amplify your voice through the square's speaker system."

The Royal Council Chair steps to the center of the platform, raising her hands for silence. The crowd gradually quiets, an expectant hush falling over the square.

"Citizens of Monrovia, distinguished guests," she begins, her voice carrying easily in the evening air. "We gather during the season of All Souls Day to cast our votes on the proposed compromise regarding Île des Lilas. Before we begin, the Duke of Atwood has informed me of a security matter that must be addressed." She turns, gesturing to where I stand. "Rebecca Orange of the Royal Investigators has requested a moment to speak."

A murmur ripples through the crowd as I make my way to the platform, Joe staying close to my side. As I climb the three short steps, I catch sight of Missy and Sacks exchanging a quick, worried glance. The Prime Minister's mustache twitches with irritation, and he reaches out to hold his wife's hand. At the edge of the crowd, Ms. Labelle crosses her arms against the chill of the wind, looking worried.

All of our suspects, in one place.

I take a deep breath, clip the microphone to my collar, and face the crowd.

"Before we vote for peace," I begin, my voice stronger than I feel, "we must solve the violence already done in its name."

The square falls completely silent. I can feel the weight of hundreds of eyes on me, but I focus on breathing, on the solid presence of Joe beside me, on the certainty of what I'm about to reveal.

"Many of you know that Ambassador Franklin was murdered during the Royal Masquerade at Castle Atwood. What you may not know is that his death was directly connected to today's vote." I pause, letting this sink in. "The Ambassador was a strong advocate for the compromise we're about to vote on—a compromise that would split Île des Lilas equally between Monrovia and Antanaro."

I glance at Jack, who gives me a slight nod of encouragement.

"Let me walk you through what happened that night," I continue. "The Masquerade was in full swing. Guests in costume mingled in the ballroom. At approximately 10:15 PM, the lights went out. When they came back on minutes later, Ambassador Franklin lay dead with a stab wound to his chest."

I move to the edge of the platform, making eye contact with different sections of the crowd as I speak.

"The first clue came from a piece of fabric. A rare, expensive yellow silk found clutched in the Ambassador's hand. This fabric was traced to Ms. Labelle's dress shop." I gesture toward Ms. Labelle, who visibly tenses. "But further investigation revealed that Ms. Labelle had made several items from this fabric— a dress for Missy Adeline, a paisley shirt for her publicist Sacks, a tie for Prime Minister Floridán, a dress for his wife Genevière, and a small purse for herself."

The Prime Minister's face reddens beneath his mustache, while Ms. Labelle wrings her hands nervously.

"At first, our investigation focused on political motives. The Prime Minister openly opposed the compromise, believing Monrovia should control the entire island." I turn to face him directly. "Your nationalist position gave you reason to want the Ambassador silenced."

The Prime Minister steps forward, his mustache practically vibrating with indignation. "This is outrageous! You have no evidence—"

"Please, Prime Minister," I interrupt. "I'm not accusing you. I'm establishing the facts."

He subsides, though his glare could melt steel.

"We also discovered that Genevière Floridán, the Prime Minister's wife, had a past romantic relationship with Ambassador Franklin— a relationship she concealed from investigators." Murmurs ripple through the crowd. "This gave her a personal connection to the victim, one strong enough that they were seen having an intense private conversation on the terrace shortly before his death."

Next to the Prime Minister, Geneviève wipes her brow. She forces a smile, but tears well in her eyes.

"It was over," she says, loudly. "It was so long ago."

"It's alright," I say, nodding. "You stayed on the terrace after you spoke to the Ambassador. Which means Geneviève was nowhere near the staircase at the time of the murder."

I shift my attention to Ms. Labelle. "While Ms. Labelle benefited financially from the publicity surrounding the 'murder fabric,' our investigation revealed she had no access to the ballroom when the lights went out. Her alibi is solid."

Relief floods Ms. Labelle's face as several people around her pat her shoulders sympathetically.

"This brings us to two other suspects who wore the yellow fabric that night: Missy Adeline and her publicist, Sacks." I turn to face them directly.

Sacks takes an involuntary step backward, while Missy maintains her composed expression, though her knuckles whiten around her clutch purse.

"It was something Jack said to me last night," I say, stepping forward. "He said, *'there's safety in numbers.'* and I realized… when the Ambassador was murdered, someone turned out the castle lights. After a quick talk with Douglas, our groundskeeper—"

I wave at Douglas, who's standing in a crowd of villagers. He gives me a gruff shrug in response.

"—I learned that the electrical breakers that control the entire castle power grid are outside in the gardens, a full five-minute walk from the ballroom where the Ambassador was murdered. Which means that someone… had an accomplice."

The crowd gasps. Murmurs echo through the square.

"We're not looking for one killer. We're looking for two," I continue, pacing in place. "Someone had to go turn out the lights, and time the movement perfectly, giving the killer a chance to stab Ambassador Franklin in the dark of the ballroom. We know that Ginevieve was still on the terrace at the opposite end of the castle at the time of the murder, which means she couldn't have aided her husband in killing the Ambassador—"

In the crowd, Prime Minister Floridàn sputters. "How dare you—I would never—"

"Which leaves," I continue. "Another pair. The movie star Missy Adeline… and her publicist, Sacks."

All eyes in the square turn to Missy, who's—quite helpfully—standing next to Sacks.

"Sacks is unaccounted for at the time of the murder. No witnesses we spoke to were able to place him in the ballroom. That's because you were in the garden, turning off the power? Isn't it, Sacks?"

Sacks throws his hands in the air. "I'm innocent! I didn't do anything!" He points a finger at Missy. "It was all her!"

Gasps emanate through the Village Square as the crowd realizes the implication of Sacks' outburst.

"Further investigation revealed that 'Sacks' isn't even his real name. He's used at least three different identities in the past decade, all connected to diplomatic events and political figures." I pause, letting the implication hang in the air. "In other words, Sacks is an intelligence operative for Antanaro."

The crowd erupts in shocked exclamations. Sacks looks around wildly, like a trapped animal searching for escape.

"They promised me they'd wipe my criminal record if I helped her and posed as her publicist!" Sacks says, frantic. "I seek clemency! Please!"

"It was also Sacks who tried to kill Jack by cutting the chandelier at the vote. But he didn't do any of this alone. He was taking orders from Missy Adeline," I press on, turning my attention to Missy. "Missy isn't just a famous actress from Antanaro. She's been photographed in disguise at numerous political events over the years— as a server, a cleaning staff member, a photographer's assistant. Always in positions that gave her access to sensitive diplomatic information."

Missy's perfect composure finally cracks, her eyes narrowing dangerously.

"In fact, Missy Adeline is also an intelligence operative—a high-ranking Antanaran agent who uses her celebrity status as the perfect cover. Who would suspect an internationally famous actress of espionage?"

Sacks suddenly breaks down, his shoulders slumping in defeat. "I couldn't say no," he blurts out, his voice cracking. "She's my boss. She ordered me to—"

"How dare you blame this on me!" Missy hisses, dropping all pretense of innocence. "You miserable, spineless, lacking in all manner of national pride—"

"It took two people to commit this murder," I interrupt, raising my voice above their argument. "One to shut down the castle lights, and one to stab the Ambassador." I turn to Sacks. "You cut the castle's power, giving Missy the darkness she needed to approach her target."

Officer Basilier moves closer to the pair, her hand resting on her holstered weapon. Two plainclothes officers emerge from the crowd, positioning themselves strategically.

"But there's one thing we still don't understand," I say, turning back to Missy. "Why kill Ambassador Franklin? He was supporting Antanaro's official position on the island compromise."

Missy's beautiful face contorts with rage and something else— frustration, perhaps, or the desperation of someone who knows they're cornered.

"Tell them, Missy," I press. "Or should I say Agent Adeline? Who did you think you were stabbing in that darkened ballroom?"

For a moment, I think she won't speak. Then, with the

dramatic flair of the trained actress she is, Missy straightens her spine and lifts her chin defiantly.

"I thought he was _him_," she spits, jerking her head toward Jack. "Same height, same build, same ridiculous salt-and-pepper hair. How was I supposed to know in the dark? The Duke was meant to die that night, not that weak, simpering, tired excuse for a diplomat!"

The crowd gasps collectively. Jack remains impassive on the platform, though I can see the slight tightening around his eyes that betrays his shock.

"Why?" I ask, though I already know the answer. "Why target the Duke?"

"Because he supports this absurd compromise!" Missy shouts, all pretense abandoned. "Île des Lilas belongs to Antanaro—all of it, not half! The research facility has discovered deposits that could change everything. Our government was too weak to demand what's rightfully ours, so I took matters into my own hands."

"What deposits?" Jack asks, speaking for the first time.

Missy's eyes gleam with a fanatic light. "Rare earth elements. And you were going to give half away for 'peace'?" She laughs bitterly. "Peace doesn't build empires."

Everything suddenly clicks into place— the desperation of their actions, the escalating violence, the willingness to attempt a public assassination. This was never just about a small island with a harbor and research station. It was about what lay beneath its surface.

"And when you realized your mistake," I continue, "when you discovered you'd killed the wrong man, you tried again with the chandelier."

"A much less subtle approach," Missy admits with chilling casualness. "But we were running out of time. The vote was imminent."

Sacks looks like he might faint, his eyes darting between

Missy and the exits. "I never wanted anyone to die," he whispers. "You said it would just be a scare tactic! A threat—"

"Shut up, you fool," Missy snaps.

In a sudden burst of movement, she shoves Sacks toward Officer Basilier and turns to run. Simultaneously, Sacks stumbles forward, knocking into a plainclothes officer who reaches for him. The crowd scatters in panic as Missy sprints toward the nearest alley, her green dress flashing like a jungle cat among the marigold decorations.

"Joe, stay!" I command, leaping from the platform to give chase. Behind me, I hear Officer Basilier's sharp commands as she coordinates officers to secure Sacks and create a perimeter.

But it's Maggie who surprises everyone. As Missy nears the alley entrance, Maggie steps directly into her path, tablet still clutched to her chest like a shield. For a split second, I think Missy will simply barrel through her— but then Maggie swings the tablet like a tennis racket, connecting solidly with the side of Missy's head.

The actress crumples to the cobblestones in an elegant heap of emerald silk.

"Administrative skills come in handy," Maggie says breathlessly as I reach them, looking down at Missy's unconscious form with a mixture of shock and satisfaction.

Officers converge on us, securing Missy with handcuffs even as she begins to stir. The crowd keeps a respectful distance, their excited chatter creating a background hum of disbelief and amazement.

I feel a hand on my shoulder and turn to find Jack standing beside me, his face a complex mixture of emotions.

"Are you alright?" he asks softly.

"Shouldn't I be asking you that?" I counter, glancing meaningfully at his injured arm. "You're the one who nearly died. Twice."

"And yet here we are," he says, his eyes crinkling at the

corners in that way that still makes my heart skip. "Both still standing."

Around us, candles continue to flicker in the evening breeze, casting dancing shadows across the cobblestones. Officer Basilier supervises as Sacks and Missy are led to separate police vehicles, their brief careers as spies and assassins officially over.

The Royal Council Chair approaches, her expression a mixture of shock and determination. "Given these... extraordinary revelations, I believe we should postpone the vote? Until we can ensure that this was the act of one rogue agent, and Antanaro had nothing to do with the crime, of course."

Jack nods in agreement. "A wise decision."

As they fall into discussion about diplomatic procedures and international protocols, I find myself stepping back, suddenly exhausted. Joe appears at my side, pressing his massive body against my leg in silent support.

"Not bad," Maggie says, joining me with her now cracked tablet still clutched in one hand. "Tell Jack I'm going to need the Castle to buy me a new tablet.

"Where did you learn to swing like that?" I ask, nodding at the cracked piece of glass in her hand.

"Tracey," Maggie says, referencing the Castle's fitness expert. The mere mention of Tracey's name sends a terrible shiver down my spine, making me think of the last painful Pilates class I allowed her to subject me to.

"She said I needed a workout that's a sport," Maggie continues. "So she's been giving me tennis lessons. Though I don't think this is what she had in mind."

We watch as the crowd begins to disperse, the excitement of the evening's drama giving way to a seasonal cheer. Music starts up from somewhere, and the scent of spiced wine and sweet pastries fills the air.

"What happens now?" Maggie asks.

"Now," I say, scratching behind Joe's ears as he leans contentedly against me, "we get back to planning a wedding."

Just then, Jack appears at my side. Despite everything—the attempts on his life, the political intrigue, the revelation of international espionage—he stands tall, already looking forward to the next adventure. "Did I hear someone say wedding?"

"I have an idea for the two of you," Maggie says slyly. "What if instead of waiting and planning and stressing about a big event, you got married on All Souls Day? Or as Rebecca calls it, Halloween?"

I blink, surprised by the suggestion. "You mean... this Halloween? As in, tomorrow night?"

"Exactly!" Maggie's enthusiasm is building. "A small, private ceremony in the Castle garden. Just family and close friends. The gardens are already decorated for the season with pumpkins and marigolds. Chef Renauld could prepare a simple but elegant dinner. And most importantly—" she pauses for emphasis, "—no time for anyone to get murdered before the ceremony!"

Jack laughs, the sound rumbling pleasantly against my side. "She makes a compelling point."

I consider the idea, picturing the castle gardens with their stone pathways lined with glowing jack-o'-lanterns, the ancient oak trees dropping golden leaves onto the lawn, the moon rising over the stone walls. It would be beautiful, intimate, perfectly us.

"All Souls Day is about magic," Maggie adds softly. "About believing in things we can't see but know are real. About connections that transcend ordinary understanding." She looks between us, her expression uncharacteristically poetic. "Isn't that what you two have?"

"Halloween in the castle garden," I say, testing the idea aloud. "With Alfredo eating pasta in the background and Joe probably trying to steal the cake."

"I'll make sure the cake is on a very high table," Maggie promises solemnly.

"The Queen might not be able to arrange travel on such short notice," Jack points out, though he doesn't sound particularly troubled by this possibility.

"We can have a reception later," I suggest, warming to the idea more with each passing second. "This would just be for us— for the people who matter most."

Jack turns to face me fully, his eyes meeting mine with such tenderness that it makes my breath catch. "Is this what you want? Truly?"

I think about all the plans we've discussed, all the royal traditions and expectations that have been weighing on us. I think about the Castle garden where we've spent so many peaceful mornings, where Joe and Luma chase each other through the roses, where Jack reads poetry to the alpacas when he thinks no one is watching. I think about Halloween —my favorite holiday— with its magic and mystery and sense of possibility.

"Yes," I say, surprising myself with how certain I feel. "I want to marry you in our garden on Halloween, with our animals and our friends, and no international incidents to interrupt."

Jack's smile is like a candle, slow and warm and full of promise. "Then that's what we'll do."

Maggie makes a small sound that might be a suppressed squeal of delight. "I'll start planning immediately. We'll need flowers, and food, and—oh! Your dress! And Jack's suit! And — oh my gosh, I need another tablet right away!"

"Breathe, Maggie," I laugh, reaching out to squeeze her arm. "It's going to be simple, remember? That's the whole point."

She inhales deeply, visibly centering herself. "Right. Simple. I can do simple." She doesn't sound entirely convinced, but her smile is genuine. "A Halloween wedding in the Castle garden. It's going to be magical."

As we turn to walk back toward the square, the last light of day giving way to the soft glow of All Souls Day candles, I feel a sense of peace settle over me. After all the chaos and danger of the past weeks, we've found our way to this moment— this decision that feels so perfectly right — it's as if it was waiting for us all along.

"Halloween," Jack murmurs beside me, testing the word. "A day for magic and mystery and new beginnings."

"And candy," I add seriously. "Don't forget the candy."

His laughter joins the music drifting from the square, a perfect harmony that feels like home.

Because some things— even in the face of murder and mayhem— remain absolutely certain.

CHAPTER
Seventeen

THANKS TO MAGGIE, the Castle garden is other-worldly. Hundreds of candles float in glass jars suspended from tree branches, their flickering flames creating dancing shadows across the stone pathways. Jack-o'-lanterns line the garden walls, their carved faces glowing with warm, orange light. Strings of marigolds form a canopy overhead, their vibrant blooms a defiant last stand against the approaching winter. I stand at the garden entrance, my heart beating so loudly I'm certain the entire castle staff can hear it. Joe sits beside me, a small velvet pouch containing our rings tied securely around his massive neck with a ribbon. He looks up at me with those wise eyes, as if to say, "Ready when you are." I take a deep breath. Who would have thought that after solving international espionage and multiple murders, getting married would be the thing that makes my knees shake?

"Stop fidgeting," Maggie whispers, adjusting the simple crown of autumn flowers she's placed in my hair. "You look perfect."

I glance down at my dress— not a traditional wedding gown but a vintage-inspired cream dress with delicate lace overlay that we miraculously found in Ms. Labelle's shop just yesterday. Now that I know she's not a murderer, getting a dress from Ms. Labelle feels like a gift. It fits like it was made for me, which Ms. Labelle insists is pure luck, but I suspect involved some overnight alterations. I'm wearing comfortable boots underneath— practical enough to walk through the village later but hidden by the hem. No way was I risking high heels on cobblestones.

"Are you sure this isn't too..." I gesture vaguely at my outfit, "casual? For marrying a Duke?"

Maggie gives me her patented don't-be-ridiculous look. "You're marrying Jack. The man who reads poetry to giraffes and has been photographed countless times with your enormous dog draped across his lap." She straightens my flower crown one final time. "Trust me, this is exactly right."

Music begins to drift through the garden— not the traditional wedding march but a haunting melody played on a single violin. Our compromise with tradition. The notes float on the cool evening air, intertwining with the scent of chrysanthemums and wood smoke.

"That's your cue," Maggie says, squeezing my hand before hurrying down the path to take her position as officiant.

Joe stands and looks at me expectantly, waiting for direction. "Okay, buddy," I whisper, taking the leash that's been decorated with tiny orange and black ribbons. "Remember what we practiced. No chasing squirrels during the ceremony."

He huffs in response, which I choose to interpret as agreement rather than negotiation.

Together, we step onto the candlelit path. The small gathering of guests turns to watch our approach, their faces glowing in the warm light of dozens of jack-o'-lanterns. I spot Chef Renauld in her formal whites, standing tall and proud beside a table laden with Halloween-themed treats. Nearby,

Monique dabs at her eyes with a lace handkerchief, her usual reserved demeanor softened by emotion. Tracey gives me an enthusiastic thumbs-up from where she stands with Enrique, who for once has abandoned his chauffeur's cap and looks almost relaxed in a formal suit. I'm grateful that our wedding is sudden—if given the chance, Tracey would try to compel me into workouts to "look my best."

The village contingent is smaller but no less invested. Jocelyn hovers near her elaborate altar of flowers and candles that she insisted on contributing. Henri stands with shoulders squared like he's about to present a prize-winning baguette, while Benjamin fidgets beside him in a suit that still has the price tag peeking out from one sleeve. Zacharia moves throughout the space, camera in hand, documenting everything with the solemnity of someone recording history.

And there, at the end of the path beneath an ancient oak tree draped with fairy lights, stands Jack. His left arm is still in a sling, a reminder of how close we came to losing everything just days ago. But his eyes— his eyes are bright and fixed on me with such naked adoration that I nearly trip over my own feet. Joe steadies me with a gentle pressure against my leg, as if he senses my momentary wobble.

Luma prances ahead of us, her role as flower girl interpreted rather liberally as she drops petals everywhere except the actual path. Her tail wags with such enthusiasm that she's creating her own little breeze, sending rose petals swirling into tiny cyclones around her paws.

As I reach Jack, Joe takes his position beside us, sitting with the dignified patience of a dog who knows he's part of something important. Jack extends his good hand to me, and I take it, feeling the warmth of his fingers intertwine with mine.

"Hi," I whisper, suddenly shy despite everything we've been through together.

"Hi yourself," he whispers back, his smile creating those

crinkles around his eyes that I love so much. "Nice night for a wedding."

"Better than a nice night for a murder," I quip before I can stop myself.

His laugh is soft but genuine. "Significantly better."

Maggie clears her throat, bringing us back to the moment. She's wearing her most formal blazer, the royal crest gleaming on the lapel. A small book rests in her hands, though I know she's memorized everything she plans to say.

"Friends, family, and four-legged companions," she begins, her voice carrying clearly through the garden. "We gather on this All Souls Night to celebrate the union of Rebecca and Jack. A night when the veil between worlds is at its thinnest seems the perfect time to join these two, who have already crossed so many boundaries together."

She pauses, looking between us with genuine affection. "Their journey to this moment has been... unconventional. Most couples meet at parties or through friends. These two met because one needed an animal expert and the other needed a job that allowed dogs the size of ponies to be by their side."

Appreciative laughter ripples through our small audience. Joe, hearing himself referenced, sits up straighter, his chest puffing out with pride.

"Most couples build their relationship through dinner dates and shared interests. These two built theirs while solving murders, surviving assassination attempts, and uncovering international espionage."

Jack squeezes my hand, his eyes never leaving mine despite Maggie's words.

"But in all those extraordinary circumstances, they discovered something very ordinary and yet infinitely precious— they found home in each other." Maggie's voice softens. "A home that transcends external labels. And that's what we celebrate tonight. Not the Duke and his animal expert, not the royal and the detective, but Jack and Rebecca—two people who choose each other, every day, no matter what challenges life throws at them. Or what chandeliers fall on them."

Another gentle wave of laughter, tinged with the collective memory of how close we came to tragedy.

"Jack and Rebecca have written their own vows, which they'll share now," Maggie continues, stepping back slightly. "Rebecca, whenever you're ready."

I take a deep breath, trying to remember the words I've been practicing in my head. But looking at Jack's face, the carefully prepared phrases slip away, leaving only the raw truth.

"Jack," I begin, my voice steadier than I expect. "A year ago, my life was shattered. I had lost my job. My relationship. And part of me wanted to stay in that place, because it was safer. But then, I was offered the job at Castle Atwood. I had no idea what waited for me on the other side, but I knew I had to be *brave*. Brave enough to try," I smile, remembering how nervous I'd been to move to Monrovia. "Now, I know what was waiting for me. It was you. And I promise to be brave with you from here on out, every day, wherever life takes us."

"Most of all, I promise to build a home with you—wherever we are, whatever we face—because home isn't Castle Atwood. Home is us."

Jack's eyes are suspiciously bright in the candlelight. He clears his throat before beginning his own vows, his voice low and intimate despite our audience.

"Rebecca," he says, and just my name in his mouth sounds like a prayer. "Before you arrived with your enormous dog and your complete disregard for royal protocol, I was going through the motions of my life. Doing what was expected, being who I was supposed to be, but never fully present."

I think of the tabloid stories I'd read about him before we met—the "party duke" with the reputation for wild living that turned out to be so different from the thoughtful man before me.

"You burst into my perfectly ordered world with chaos and curiosity and an unwavering moral compass. You saw through the title to the person beneath, and you challenged me to be better— not as a Duke, but as a human being. I love my country. I love my duties. But from this moment on, I promise to keep *you* as the center of the world, as my first and deepest love."

There's a collective sigh from our audience, and I'm pretty sure I hear Monique quietly sobbing. Even Henri's mustache seems to quiver with emotion.

"The rings, please," Maggie prompts gently.

This is Joe's big moment. He stands up, every inch the dignified ring bearer, and takes one solemn step forward. Then Luma, overcome with excitement, darts between his legs, sending him off-balance. The velvet pouch swings precariously from his neck. For one heart-stopping moment, I think our rings are about to go flying into the darkness.

But Joe recovers with surprising grace for a dog his size, steadying himself and giving Luma a look that clearly says, "Not now, amateur." She subsides, appropriately chastened, and sits beside Maggie with her tail still thumping against the garden path.

Maggie carefully unties the pouch from Joe's neck, retrieving the two simple bands we chose together—white gold for Jack, rose gold for me, both engraved inside with the same message: "For adventures yet to come."

Jack takes my ring, sliding it onto my finger with a steady hand despite his injured arm. "With this ring, I thee wed," he says, the traditional words somehow fresh and new in his voice.

I take his ring in turn, gently sliding it onto his finger. "With this ring, I thee wed," I echo, amazed at how such simple words can carry so much meaning.

"By the authority vested in me by the Royal Registry of Monrovia," Maggie says, her voice ringing clear in the night air, "I now pronounce you husband and wife, Duke and Duchess of Atwood." She grins, adding, "You may now kiss your bride, preferably before any international incidents interrupt."

Jack laughs, then leans in to kiss me. It's gentle at first, mindful of our audience, but deepens into something that feels like a promise, like coming home. When we finally break apart, our small gathering erupts in applause and cheers. Joe barks enthusiastically, his deep voice echoing through the garden. Even Luma joins in, yipping excitedly and running circles around us.

"May I present," Maggie announces over the celebration, "Their Graces, the Duke and Duchess of Atwood!"

"Or as they prefer," Zacharia calls out, camera still clicking away, "Jack and Rebecca, Royal Investigators!"

More cheers follow as we make our way back down the path, hand in hand, Joe and Luma prancing ahead of us. The reception is simple but perfect— Chef Renauld's Halloween-themed treats arranged on tiered stands, glasses of champagne (and water bowls for the dogs), and a small cake topped with miniature figures of us, complete with tiny versions of Joe and Luma at our feet.

"The photos will be ready tomorrow," Zacharia tells us as we sample the pumpkin-spiced cake. "I'll create a special spread for the village bulletin, just enough to make everyone feel included without compromising your privacy."

"Thank you," Jack says sincerely. "It's the perfect compromise."

"Speaking of including everyone," I say, glancing at the large baskets waiting near the garden entrance, "is it time for the next part of our celebration?"

Jack's eyes light up. "Absolutely."

Even though Jack and I decided to have a private ceremony, I still wanted to include the public. And I've thought of the perfect way to do it.

We gather our guests and explain the plan— a procession into the village, handing out candies and small treats to celebrate not just our wedding but the blending of our traditions: my American Halloween customs with Monrovia's All Souls Day observances.

"In America, children go 'trick-or-treating' on Halloween," I explain as Jack and Enrique distribute the baskets among our group. "Since we've decided to get married on this night, we thought it would be fun to reverse the tradition— we'll go to the villagers and offer treats as a way of sharing our joy."

"And for thanking the villagers who have put up with our detective work disrupting village life on multiple occasions," Maggie adds with a grin.

Our procession moves from the Castle down to the Village, lanterns lighting our way. The night is crisp but not cold, perfect for walking. We look like some strange Halloween parade— formal attire mixed with baskets of candy, two dogs leading the way, trailing flower petals and ribbons.

The village square is still decorated for All Souls Day, marigolds and candles creating a golden glow across the cobblestones. As word spreads of our approach, people emerge from homes and shops, gathering to greet us.

"Congratulations!" they call. Children run up eagerly when they spot our candy baskets.

"Happy Halloween!" I call back, handing out treats and accepting well-wishes. "Happy All Souls Day!"

Jack moves through the crowd with natural grace, kneeling to offer candy to children despite his injured arm, accepting handshakes and congratulations with genuine warmth. Joe and Luma become instant celebrities, patient with little hands that want to pet them, accepting scratches and compliments with canine dignity.

"Quite a different scene from the last time we were all gathered here," Maggie observes as we watch Jack charming an elderly couple who've lived in the village their entire lives. "Less spy-chasing, more celebration.

"Though equally exhausting," I admit, feeling the weight of the day's emotions. "In the best possible way."

The celebration continues well into the night, the Village's All Souls Day traditions blending seamlessly with our wedding festivities. There's dancing in the square, more of Chef Renauld's treats distributed among the crowd, and even Henri contributes fresh-baked bread shaped like wedding rings.

As midnight approaches, Jack finds me near the village fountain, where I've sat down to rest for a moment. Joe lies at my feet, equally tired from all the attention and excitement.

"Duchess," Jack says, sliding onto the bench beside me.

"That's going to take some getting used to," I admit, leaning against his shoulder.

"We have time," he says, pressing a kiss to my temple. "A lifetime, in fact."

"A lifetime of royal duties and animal care and probably at least a few more murders to solve," I muse, watching the candlelight flicker across the square where villagers still celebrate.

"Speaking of," Jack says with a mischievous glint in his eye, "I've arranged for our honeymoon to be completely murder-free. Signed agreements from all potential victims and everything."

I laugh, the sound mixing with the distant music. "Well, that's a relief. I'd hate for my first official act as Duchess to be solving another case."

"I wouldn't mind," Jack says, his voice suddenly serious.

I turn to look at him, this remarkable man who has become my husband. In the glow of All Souls Day candles, with the distant sounds of celebration surrounding us and Joe snoring gently at our feet, I feel a sense of rightness so profound it takes my breath away.

"I love you," I tell him simply. "Murders or no murders."

"I love you too," he replies, leaning in to kiss me. "For all our adventures yet to come."

A Poisonous Play

Being a duchess, it turns out, is significantly more nerve-wracking than wrangling wildlife. I think the words while sitting in the front row of Monrovia's Grand Playhouse, wearing an *actual* tiara while two hundred pairs of eyes burn holes into the back of my neck. The velvet seat beneath me feels too hard, and I resist the urge to check if my formal gown is riding up in the back.

"You're fidgeting," Jack whispers, his breath warm against my ear as he reaches over to place his hand on mine, stilling my fingers that have been unconsciously pleating the program into accordion folds.

"I'm not fidgeting. I'm... reinterpreting the structural integrity of paper," I whisper back, but I let the mangled program rest in my lap. "Everyone is staring."

"Of course they're staring. Look at you." Jack's eyes crinkle at the corners as he smiles at me, that private smile that still makes my stomach flip even after months of marriage. "You're the most beautiful woman in the world."

"I'm the most *terrified* woman in the world," I correct him, though I can't help the warmth that spreads through me at his words.

Beside me, Joe shifts his massive frame, the bow tie around his thick neck looking comically small against his golden fur. He lets out a small huff, clearly unimpressed with having to sit still for so long. On Jack's other side, Luma, his elegant collie, sits primly in her sparkly collar, the picture of canine dignity.

"Joe, please behave," I murmur, leaning down to straighten his bow tie. "This is our first official royal outing as a family."

"He looks very distinguished," Maggie says from my other side, her blonde braids elaborately woven with tiny pearls for the occasion. "Like he's about to deliver a TED Talk on the superiority of bacon treats."

I snort, earning a disapproving glance from an elderly woman two rows back. *Great.* Five minutes into my first official event as a royal patron and I'm already committing some faux pas. I can see tomorrow's headlines now: "New Duchess Snorts Like Barnyard Animal at Shakespeare Opening.

The Grand Playhouse of Monrovia is every bit as impressive as its name suggests. The building had been lovingly restored over the past year, with its ornate gold-leaf ceiling medallions and plush red velvet seats making it feel like we've stepped back in time to a more elegant era. Crystal chandeliers hang overhead, their light catching and refracting in the jewels adorning the necks and wrists of Monrovia's elite. The air smells of polished wood, expensive perfume, and the faint, exciting whiff of fresh paint from the newly renovated stage.

My gaze travels up to the royal box— where we should be sitting, according to tradition— but Jack had insisted we take front-row seats with the people instead. "If we're going to support the arts," he'd said, "let's actually see the arts up close." It was one of the many reasons I'd fallen in love with him— his determination to modernize without destroying tradition, to be part of the community rather than floating above it.

I smooth down the front of my emerald green gown, trying to look like I belong here. The tiara— a small, tasteful one from the royal collection that Jack had insisted I wear— feels like it weighs a thousand pounds, though it can't be more than a few ounces. I'd practiced walking with it for hours, terrified I'd send it tumbling to the ground in front of everyone.

"Relax," Jack whispers again, his fingers giving mine a gentle squeeze. "You're doing brilliantly."

"I haven't done anything yet except sit here looking petrified."

"That's basically the entire job. You're nailing it," he teases, his eyes twinkling.

I resist the urge to elbow him in the ribs, aware that such behavior is probably frowned upon in duchesses. Instead, I take a deep breath and try to center myself. This playhouse means something to me. It's not just a building; it's a statement about the importance of arts and culture, of stories that connect us across centuries. When Jack had asked what cause I wanted to champion as a duchess, I hadn't hesitated.

"I still think we should have gone on our honeymoon first," Jack says, voice pitched low enough that only I can hear him. "Paris in the spring, Rome in the summer— we could have done the whole grand tour before diving into official duties."

"And leave Monrovia without quality Shakespeare for another six months?" I reply, arching an eyebrow. "I couldn't stand the thought of it. Besides, the dogs would have missed us."

As if on cue, Joe lets out a dramatic sigh and slumps against my leg, his furry head resting heavily on my foot. Even in formal attire, he's still my oversized, lovable goofball.

"He's not wrong about the honeymoon, though," Maggie

chimes in, leaning forward to look past me at Jack. "Most royal brides would milk that for all it's worth. Three weeks minimum in some exotic locale, Instagram photos on yachts, drinking mimosas for breakfast..."

"Thank you for that helpful input, Maggie," I say dryly.

She grins. "Just saying, most women wouldn't rush back to work quite so quickly after marrying a duke.

"Well, I'm not most women," I reply, thinking quietly that Maggie is probably right. I jumped into being a royal too quickly, maybe because I felt I had something to prove. Now, I'm a patron of the theater, and I feel totally unprepared.

"Rebecca is a force that can't be stopped," Jack agrees, his voice warm with pride. "Truthfully, I'm not surprised at all."

"Neither am I," Maggie says, her smile softening.

"If I don't end up in the papers tonight, I'll consider my efforts a win," I say.

"Rebecca," Maggie shakes her head. "You *always* end up in the papers one way or another."

Before I can defend myself, the house lights begin to dim. The murmur of conversation around us fades as the audience settles in. Joe shifts against my leg, and I reach down to place a calming hand on his massive head. For all his size and occasional clumsiness, he understands the concept of quiet time remarkably well.

"I still can't believe they chose 'The Taming of the Shrew' for their opening production," Jack whispers to me as the lights continue to lower. "It's not exactly the most progressive of Shakespeare's works."

"The director mentioned something about a modern reinterpretation," I whisper back. "I hope they pull it off. Otherwise, the papers will say it's my fault. In fact, anything that goes wrong tonight will be my fault."

The final lights dim, plunging the theater into a moment of perfect darkness before a single spotlight illuminates the heavy red curtains. My heart beats faster with anticipation.

Whatever my misgivings about the play choice, there's something magical about this moment— the hush of expectation, the collective held breath of an audience about to be transported.

The curtains part with a soft whoosh, revealing a tavern scene that serves as the play's opening. The set design is impressive—weathered wooden tables, flickering lantern light, and a sense of lived-in authenticity that immediately establishes the world of the play. A man in tattered clothing sprawls across one of the benches, clearly meant to be Christopher Sly, the drunken tinker from the play's induction.

"I'll pheeze you, in faith," the actor slurs, staggering to his feet as the tavern hostess approaches.

The actress playing the hostess is magnificent— her exasperation palpable as she confronts Sly about his drunken behavior and unpaid tab. Their exchange is sharp and funny, drawing appreciative chuckles from the audience. I find myself leaning forward slightly, drawn into the performance despite my earlier reservations.

It's going so well, I think, struck by a moment of pride. *Why was I worried? My first royal patronage is going to be perfect.*

The actor playing Sly lurches around the stage with impressive physical comedy, his movements just controlled enough to show the skill behind the apparent chaos. When he reaches for his tankard on the table, his timing is perfect— a dramatic pause, a wobbling reach, and then a firm grasp that draws another laugh from the audience.

"A sixpence a piece, and I'll pay you!" he announces grandly, lifting the tankard for a deep, theatrical swig. The actor swallows.

Then, he pauses. For a second, I think he's forgotten his lines.

Something changes in his expression. The tankard slips from his fingers, clattering to the stage floor. His body follows a moment later, crumpling in a way that doesn't look rehearsed.

The audience laughs— they think the fall is part of the comedy, a drunken collapse played for laughs. But I've seen enough animals in distress to recognize when something is terribly wrong. The man's face has gone slack in a way that has nothing to do with acting. His limbs aren't positioned to protect himself from the fall—they're completely limp.

Something's wrong with him, I think. I want to tell everyone, but the words get stuck in my throat.

The actress playing the hostess continues her lines for a moment before she seems to realize something's amiss. She approaches the fallen actor.

"Christopher?" she says his character's name. When he doesn't respond, she kneels beside him, her hand on his shoulder, more frantic now. "Tom?" This time using what must be the actor's real name. "*Tom,* are you alright?"

The audience begins to murmur, the atmosphere in the theater shifting from amusement to uncertainty. Joe senses it too, his massive head lifting from my foot as he sits up straighter. Beside him, Luma growls, raising the fur on her back.

The actress's face changes as she rolls the actor onto his back, revealing his unnaturally pale face. "Someone get help!" she calls out, her voice piercing through the confused murmurs of the audience. "He's not breathing!"

Beside me, Jack leans close. "Was that part of the show?" he asks, his voice tight with concern.

I'm already half-rising from my seat, my eyes fixed on the fallen actor. There's a familiar stillness to him that sends a chill down my spine.

"I don't think so," I reply, my voice barely above a whisper. "I think... he's been *poisoned.*"

The word seems to hang in the air between us as chaos erupts on stage. The curtain begins to lower hastily, but not before we see several stagehands rushing toward the fallen actor. A woman in the third row screams, and suddenly the orderly theater dissolves into panicked confusion.

Joe presses against my leg, his training kicking in as he senses my tension. Luma whines softly from Jack's side. Maggie is already on her phone, presumably calling for medical assistance.

I meet Jack's eyes, seeing my own shock reflected there. Our perfect opening night— my first official function as duchess and patron— has just become something else entirely.

So much for not ending up in the papers, I think.

———

To keep reading, look for "A Poisonous Play," available in paperback!

More From Valerie Brandy

The Rebecca Orange Castle Cozy Mystery Series:

1. Mystery at Monrovia Castle
2. A Victim in the Village
3. A Royal Ruse
4. A Kidnapped Collie
5. A Perilous Proposal
6. Murder at the Masquerade
7. A Poisonous Play

The Private Investigator Annie Hudson Mystery Series:

1. Murder Behind the Gates
2. Murder in the Penthouse
3. Murder on the Farm
4. Murder in the Commune
5. Murder in the Desert
6. Murder in the Hometown

The Predator / Prey Thriller Series:

1. Trail of Obsession
2. Lies Run Deep
3. The Trap is Set
4. Woman in the Wind

Dear Reader,

Thank you for dedicating your time to the world of Monrovia and Rebecca Orange! These books mean so much to me, and my hope is always that what I've written gives you the chance to escape to a cozy new place.

I love hearing from readers (seriously, it makes the job so fun!). Please reach out to me anytime by visiting www.valeriebrandy.com or finding me on social media, even if it's just to say "hi" or talk about flower names for coffee. Monrovia is special because of the community there, and I love forming the same cozy friendships around my books.

You can also join my author club mailing list for free give-aways and updates on new releases. Scan the QR Code below or visit my website to join!

Warmly,

— Valerie Brandy

www.ingramcontent.com/pod-product-compliance
Lightning Source LLC
Chambersburg PA
CBHW071308030726
47594CB00002B/350